Praise for Karis Walsh

Sit. Stay. Love.

"A cute and fun romance set in a small town. Great main characters that are easily relatable."—*Kat Adams, Bookseller (QBD Books, Australia)*

"This is a sweet romance about two lovely people growing together and falling in love as they help the people and animals around them."—*Rainbow Reflections*

"This is an easy romance to read. It's not overly fraught with angst, but there is some light drama to keep the plot moving forward. The obligatory separation of the leads near the end of the book didn't feel eye-roll worthy, because, though dramatic, it was set up almost from the beginning of the book. I loved the characters, pacing and plot of this book. Very recommended."—*Colleen Corgel, Librarian, Queens Public Library*

Love on Lavender Lane

"Gentle romance, excellent chemistry and low angst…The two MCs are well defined and well written. Their interactions and dialogue are great fun. The whole atmosphere of the lavender farm is excellently evoked."—*reviewer@large*

Love on Lavender Lane "was very nearly my perfect romance novel. Lovely human beings for main characters who had fantastic chemistry, great humor that kept me smiling—and even laughing—throughout, and just enough angst to make me feel it in the heart. And a cute doggie, too!"—*C-Spot Reviews*

Seascape

"When I think of Karis Walsh novels, the two aspects that distinguish them from those of many authors are the interactions of the characters with their environment, both the scenery and the plants and animals that live in it. This book has all of that in abundance."—*The Good, the Bad and the Unread*

T0019002

Set the Stage

"I really adored this book. From the characters to the setting and the slow burn romance, I was in it for the long haul with this one. Karis Walsh to me is an expert in creating interesting characters that often have to face some type of adversity. While this book was no different, it felt like the author changed up her game a bit. There was something new, something fresh about this book from Walsh."
—*Romantic Reader Blog*

"Both leads were well developed and you could see them grow as characters throughout the novel. They also had great chemistry. This slow burn romance made a great summer read."—*Melina Bickard, Librarian, Waterloo Library (UK)*

Amounting to Nothing

"As always with Karis Walsh's books, the characters are well drawn and the inter-relationships well developed."—*Lesbian Reading Room*

Tales from Sea Glass Inn

"*Tales from Sea Glass Inn* is a lovely collection of stories about the women who visit the Inn and the relationships that they form with each other."—*Inked Rainbow Reads*

Blindsided

"Their slow-burn romance is a nuanced exploration of trust, desire, and negotiating boundaries, without a hint of schmaltz or pity. The sex scenes are sizzling hot, but it's the slow burn that really allows Walsh to shine...the deft dialogue and well-written characters make this a winner."—*Publishers Weekly*

"This is definitely a good read, and it's a good introduction to Karis Walsh and her books. The romance is good, the sex is hot, the dogs are endearing, and you finish the book feeling good. Why wouldn't you want all that?"—*Lesbian Review*

By the Author

Harmony

Worth the Risk

Sea Glass Inn

Improvisation

Mounting Danger

Wingspan

Blindsided

Mounting Evidence

Love on Tap

Tales from Sea Glass Inn

Amounting to Nothing

You Make Me Tremble

Set the Stage

Seascape

Love on Lavender Lane

Sit. Stay. Love.

Liberty Bay

LIBERTY BAY

by

Karis Walsh

2021

LIBERTY BAY

ISBN 13: 978-1-63555-816-6

THIS TRADE PAPERBACK ORIGINAL IS PUBLISHED BY
BOLD STROKES BOOKS, INC.
P.O. BOX 249
VALLEY FALLS, NY 12185

FIRST EDITION: JANUARY 2021

CREDITS
EDITOR: RUTH STERNGLANTZ
PRODUCTION DESIGN: STACIA SEAMAN
COVER DESIGN BY TAMMY SEIDICK

LIBERTY BAY

CHAPTER ONE

Gina Strickland used her fork to push the sliced strawberries on her plate into an even, bright red arc that framed the slice of vegetable quiche. The meal seemed to her to be a boring subject for a photo—even though it smelled delicious—but she took the obligatory picture of the food before she started eating. All around her, at over a dozen round tables in the department store's meeting room, the other diners were doing the exact same thing.

Conversations faded as the lunch attendees concentrated on devouring the meal, but the room was far from silent. Constant pings and chimes from all the phones in the room—Gina's included—provided an auditory backdrop to the more sporadic scrapes of utensils against china. Gina appreciated the reprieve from small talk as she focused both on the quiche and on the exhausting mental comparison of everyone's notifications. The sounds could mean anything from new followers to page views to emails from friends, but influencing was a numbers game at heart, and she was relieved to hear that she was holding her own.

There were a few heavy hitters in the room, as well as some new names, but most of the guests invited to this PR reception for one of Seattle's large downtown department stores were micro-influencers like Gina. She was on the higher end of the spectrum, hovering in the space where the *micro* modifier could potentially be dropped and always hoping for the next viral story that would raise her viewership over the five hundred thousand mark, though her income was still inconsistent and not something she could take for granted yet. As much as these events made her uncomfortable, she was not about to turn down the chance to make some new connections and to vie for sponsorships. Not to mention the free lunch.

After the meal and presentation were finished, she wandered around the room along with her peers, taking pictures of the various products being showcased by the store. She was sure everyone was feeling the same pressure to take their nearly identical photos of uninspired quiche, kitchen appliances, and designer jeans and turn them magically into a unique photo story that would draw page views like a magnet. In between camera shots, she carried on what felt to her like intimate conversations with people she barely knew. Even though she was starting to make a very successful career out of her lifestyle blogs and posts, she still felt a jolt of surprise when near strangers approached her and started chatting about her wardrobe or the choice of lamps she had chosen for her bedroom.

She had made the decision to invite the internet into her life, so complaints or the response *That's none of your business* weren't options for her. Still, for someone who felt awkward talking with other people about even innocuous topics such as the weather, such leaps into personal territory often made her uncomfortable. She interacted with thousands of people on social media platforms on a daily basis, and she had plenty of opportunities to turn those interactions into friendships or romantic relationships, but she still hadn't figured out how to cope with the way relationships that started online leaped with dizzying speed into familiarity when they transferred to real life. She preferred to keep her close friendships safely in the virtual world while holding part of herself at a distance when in person.

Gina took a picture of a pair of shoes in a horrid shade of green, then immediately deleted it since it would never find its way onto any of her social media sites. Once she had built her following just a little more, pushing herself into consistent six-figure views, she would be able to rely less on these mass receptions. She would be invited to more personal lunches with PR representatives and would be able to tailor sponsorships so they aligned even more closely with her interests and tastes than they did now. She didn't think the conversations would be any less uncomfortable at those one-on-one meetings than they were in these large groups, but the opportunities for monetizing her platforms would expand.

Once the reception ended, she caught a bus just outside the store for the short trip back to her apartment, wedging the unexpectedly bulky PR gifts between her knees and the seat in front of her. The comforter would be a beautiful addition to her bedroom, which was the next room in line to be decorated. The designer handbag, with its numerous buckles and logos, was not her style at all, but it would make a great giveaway item for her viewers.

She leaned back against the seat and closed her eyes during the ride, soothed by the alerts from her phone, which were coming more and more frequently now—one or more of her posts must be blowing up today. As much as she was relieved to be out of the reception room and away from all the people and necessary chatting, she was grateful for the swag and for the increased revenue she was going to gain after connecting with the PR representative during their brief interchange before the meal. Not a bad reward for a mere two hours of her time and a measly five-minute bus ride from her home.

❖

Gina moved the black feather half an inch to the left, nestling it more deeply in a fold of silky white fabric. She stood and peered through the viewfinder again. Perfect. She took several shots before she was satisfied with the composition of her photo, and then she swiftly dismantled the scene she had spent over an hour planning and tweaking. The feather and pale blue glass beads were stowed in their appropriate tiny drawers in the cabinet she had bought for less than ten dollars at a garage sale and refinished until it looked worth many times that amount, all thoroughly documented as the inspiration for her series of videos on home decorating on a strict budget. She put her favorite cinnamon and honey scented candle back on the matching bookshelf—project number two in the same series—and set the book which had been the focal point of her picture on her bedside table. She folded the backdrop cloth and decorative swatches of antique lace and tucked them into a plastic bin with a tight-fitting cover meant to keep her hoard of beautiful fabric protected and from turning into a mess of strings and tatters. She had learned that lesson the hard way, when she hadn't bothered to tidy up after a shoot and had snagged a vintage piece of brocade with her vacuum cleaner where it lay forgotten on the floor.

Her phone was still sending nearly constant—and nearly irresistible—alerts her way, but she forced herself to ignore it until her work was done. She had five photo stories to edit and upload before she would allow herself to be distracted by messages and viewer comments, no matter how tempting and numerous they sounded. Plus, she usually found these extended photo sessions to be a good way to decompress after the stress of spending an afternoon at a real-life social event. The work calmed her and reminded her why she loved her career, with its creative challenges and opportunities for connecting with her followers.

She poured a cup of strong Assam tea and sat at her kitchen table where her laptop, paper-filled binders, and overflowing planner took up most of the space. She downloaded the day's shots and worked through the pictures one by one. The book she was reading. The ingredients for her healthy morning smoothie. Her weekly planner spread and her monthly budget template. A set of close-ups of flowers and leaves for a post about city living on a new platform she was trying called Unify. She ignored the twinge of guilt she felt because her city-nature walk had really been nothing more than the quick trip home from the bus stop, as she had struggled to snap some suitable pictures while keeping the comforter and purse from touching the ground. And after twenty irritable minutes spent wrangling rolling berries and discolored banana slices this morning, she had tossed her lovely smoothie ingredients into the fridge and instead had eaten a bowl of Lucky Charms for breakfast. She tried to keep her content genuine, but some days, her real life demanded easier, less photogenic choices. Still, chipped bowls of sugary cereal weren't going to get as many views as artistically arranged rainbows of fruits and greens.

She shifted in her chair and bumped the card table with her knee, sloshing tea out of her mug and onto her pile of to-do lists. She swore quietly, mopping up the liquid with the sleeve of her sweatshirt and spreading the pages out on the table to dry. She pulled off the damp shirt and tossed it in the general direction of her bedroom, finishing her adjustments to color saturation in a sports bra. Once she was done, she made a note on one of her lists to look for a cheap but sturdy desk. She chewed on the end of her pen and watched the ink bleed on the damp paper before adding a list of other topics that could turn the hunt for a desk into a few months' worth of blogs about setting up and running a home office.

She glanced around her apartment, looking for inspiration. She concentrated most of her decorating efforts and furniture budget on one area at a time, and only filmed in those completed locations, giving her apartment a blotchy effect as some parts were fit for a magazine photo shoot while other spaces—such as where she ate and worked—had a flimsy, temporary feel. When she started fixing up a zone, she had to make it earn its keep. No small detail, from choosing a paint color to stenciling a rustic wooden picture frame, was completed unless it had a photo spread, DIY video, or blog post to go along with it.

Luckily, her apartment was small enough—and cheap enough—to give her hope that she would eventually finish decorating the entire place. If she had a higher rent to pay, she'd have even smaller zones of beauty and tranquility than she had now, since she refused to use more than a few sponsored products in each one. She wanted her posts to resonate with her viewers, and most of them were on a budget and didn't have stores handing them free merchandise. Gina would rather slowly make the space her own, sharing her inspiration and methods with her followers, rather than turning it into an imitation of a department store showroom. She appreciated the pockets of charm in her home because they reflected who she was.

When she had first come to Seattle, she had toured apartment buildings with rents comparable to mortgage payments for large homes on acreage in her old hometown near Moses Lake, in eastern Washington. She had vowed she was never—*never*—going back there, no matter how cheap the cost of living, even if she had to resort to sharing a studio apartment with cockroaches and three roommates. It hadn't come to that, though, since the new online connections she was forming while she stayed in a musty hotel on the outskirts of the city brought her to this early 1900 Craftsman with its tiny back wing and private entrance. The space had been a blank canvas when she moved in, and she had started making it her own by decorating the living room. She had posted a few photos of her progress on Instagram on a whim, never expecting viewers to flock to her site by the hundreds. By the time she had put the finishing touches on the room, those numbers were in the thousands, and her side hobby had become her full-time job.

Gina and the owners of the house were on friendly enough terms to wave and say hello, but not enough to invite each other over for meals or chitchat, which suited her quite well. Beacon Hill was far enough from the trendier neighborhoods to be somewhat affordable, yet close enough to downtown for her to have easy access whenever she needed to attend one of her frequent PR events. The heterogenous mix of people living around her gave Gina the anonymity and variety she craved from daily life in a big city, while the relationships she had formed with sponsors had helped connect her online presence to the city.

Her phone continued to ping, insistent in its attempts to keep her from work. Her schedule was as compartmentalized as her home, though, and filming and uploading always came before social time. Her priority was paying for her life in Seattle. Enjoying that life had to come second. She pushed her phone farther away and opened one of her thick binders instead, pulling out her notes from a recent visit to a new local Vietnamese restaurant and writing a review for her *Living and Eating in Beacon Hill* blog. Once it was posted, she sketched out a script for a video she planned to film for her urban lifestyle channel on creating a natural sanctuary in small city gardens. Gina loved sitting in gardens and hated digging in them, but luckily, her landlord had a beautiful yard complete with vegetables, newly budding fruit trees, and colorful spring tulips. An ornate wrought iron bench would make a perfect place for filming the urban retreat. Gina mentally reviewed the way she planned to decorate it with throw pillows and a tray of coffee and croissants as she finally reached for her phone.

She wasn't surprised to see Maia's name repeatedly listed under missed calls. While Gina couldn't let herself be sidetracked from work or she'd lose focus, Maia seemed to thrive on multitasking. She called or texted while she was doing other things, sharing snippets of her life and scraps of newly forming ideas with Gina even though she knew answers wouldn't come until Gina's allotted rest time. For all of her thousands of followers and acquaintances across the social media world, Maia was one of the very few who shared a more personal relationship with Gina. The fact that Maia lived in Nashville and they had never met in person didn't change the fierce way Gina loved her friend.

Instead of listening to Maia's voice mails or reading the texts, Gina sent a request to videochat, hoping Maia was at a good enough stopping point in one of her many projects to be able to talk. Sure enough, her image popped onto Gina's screen almost immediately.

Gina had felt buoyant, prepared to share whatever good news was happening on her sites with her friend, but she felt her smile fade in an instant. Maia looked like her normal workday self, with expert makeup and her tightly curled hair coiled into perfect ringlets, but Gina knew from her tense expression that something was wrong and launched into questions, forgoing any traditional greetings and pushing aside her curiosity about her own online situation.

"Are you okay? Did something happen?"

Maia shook her head slightly. "I'm fine. But you haven't checked any of your socials yet, have you."

The latter was spoken as a statement of fact, not a question, and Gina felt her stomach clench with tension. Maia was okay, but somehow Gina herself wasn't. She had been certain the volume of alerts from her phone was a positive signal—numbers were good, weren't they? The higher the better. She pulled her laptop in front of her again and opened YouTube to her most recent video. A cursory glance showed her subscriber number holding steady. So far, so good. "No, I haven't. I just posted some photos, and I was going to respond to comments after lunch. What is…oh, fuck."

"Yep," Maia agreed. "Fuck is the right word."

Gina lowered her phone while she blinked through a haze of disbelief and read the comments raging across the page. She was vaguely aware that Maia probably had an angled view of her fridge now, but she felt too weak to continue holding the phone at face level.

She was accustomed to rude comments by now—no one who was in the social media spotlight could escape them—but she'd never experienced anything like the venom in these posts. Even on a good day, her face, her hair, her voice, all were considered fair game by a small minority of the followers who watched her videos or saw her posts and pictures. Those comments were sometimes hurtful, sometimes too ridiculous to merit more than a roll of the eyes, but all were survivable. Was this survivable?

Her address, her license plate and make and color of her car, a list of places where she did her banking and shopping. Her social security number. The public display of those personal details was bad enough, but the inciting statements were so much worse. Threats to hurt her, burn down her house, and more were spelled out in graphic detail. Disbelief warred with a tremor of primal fear, and the time when she had been concerned about the placement of feathers or the layout of a pretty coffee tray seemed so far away as to belong to a different lifetime, not a mere five minutes before.

"What do I…How can I…" Gina's voice faded away, as she was unable to articulate her questions, let alone decide on a course of action. She was familiar with doxing, of course, but only in an abstract way. As something that happened to other people, to bigger names, but not as something that would ever happen to her. Her fingers, usually so confident and comfortable as they connected her to her online world, hovered over the keyboard with uncertainty.

"Don't just delete them," Maia's voice warned, as if anticipating Gina's instinct to make the comments disappear.

Gina lifted the phone again and took some comfort from Maia's sympathetic expression. "I can't leave them," she argued.

Maia shook her head. "Remove the comments from view but take screenshots and report this. It's all on Instagram and Unify, too. Just don't get rid of any evidence, just in case."

"In case *what*?" Gina asked, cringing at the note of terror she heard in her voice. "In case someone really tries to…do any of those horrible things to me?"

"Just be smart. Keep the evidence and clean up your accounts. Close the threads so no one else can post comments until you're ready for them."

Gina sat still, numbed by the thought of how many accounts she had that might be compromised. How many tendrils of herself she had spread across the internet that might have been infected. Wouldn't it be better to quit and delete her accounts? Find something else to do, some other way to make a living. But what could possibly replace this world she had worked so hard to build?

"Gina, stop," Maia said, as if aware of the thoughts rampaging through Gina's mind. "Put me down on the table and get this done. I'll be right here with you the whole time."

Gina managed a brief nod, and then she set her phone down and got to work. With Maia calling out encouragement and advice, Gina steadily slogged through the violent words on her screen, capturing every hateful comment, submitting detailed formal reports to each site's admin hosts, and changing her settings to keep new posts from appearing while she struggled to remove the ones already there. As her mind started to clear, she was able to recognize the initial doxer's screenname as someone she had conversed with briefly in the comments section of an earlier video. One of the dozens of followers who thought they knew her well enough to want to meet in person, hinting at a relationship she knew was never going to happen. She had responded in what she believed was a friendly way, clearly setting a boundary around her private life, but apparently this person had been more offended than she would have thought possible by her refusal. She searched for the original interaction and added it to her growing list of screenshots.

With each keystroke, she felt a sliver of her fear chip away and get replaced by a cold shard of anger. By the time she had finished, when neither she nor Maia could find any more threats to eradicate, Gina felt as if her formerly terrorized self had been replaced cell by cell. She shook out her fingers and clenched her hands into tight fists, not sure if the tingling sensation she felt was due to her furious typing or the fury coursing through her.

The phone trembled in her hand when she picked it up so she and Maia could see each other again. She braced her other hand against her wrist to keep the cell's camera steady.

"Why would someone do this to me?" Gina asked. "I live

in a tiny apartment and write about books and gardens and how to paint old bookshelves. Having me turn down a date can't be such a big deal—it's not like I'm a celebrity."

"Well, you are, in a way, although that doesn't give anyone the right to dox you. This person probably thought they meant something to you and got angry when you made it clear you didn't feel the same way. Unfortunately, the anonymity of the internet gives cowards the ability to say things they'd never say in person."

"So you don't think I need to overreact?" Gina asked, sagging in her chair with relief. She had initially been ready to run away, but she couldn't let one cruel person take away the unconventional career she had worked hard to develop. The internet was her home, maybe even more than this apartment. It was the only place where she felt safe and free to express herself without the awkwardness she felt when she came out from behind the computer screen. Where she *had* felt safe, she amended internally. "I'll be more careful from now on and check my comments all the time. I can set up the comments so I can review them before—"

"Stop," Maia said. "I said the person probably wouldn't follow through on their threats, not that they definitely wouldn't. Or that another person might not read what they posted and try to hurt you. You need to take this seriously and get somewhere safe. Out of the city."

"Leave my home?" Gina asked, stunned by the vehemence in Maia's voice. She wasn't sure which would be worse, having to leave Seattle and the apartment she adored or erasing her online presence. Both were too tied to who she was to be easily severed from her life.

"Kirk and I talked about it, and we'd like to have you come here and stay with us for a while. Spend as long as you want with us and look for a place of your own if you decide to stay in Tennessee. You'd love Nashville."

Gina sat in stunned silence as Maia enumerated the many great qualities and attractions available in Nashville. Her speech had a slightly rehearsed sound to it, and Gina guessed she had been working on it all morning while she tried in vain to reach Gina. The idea tempted her more than it should—an entire unknown city to explore, with plenty of opportunities for fresh photo stories and video ideas. A friend nearby to help her bear this awful and unexpected burden of hate that had been dropped on her shoulders. Her mind ventured a few yards down the path of planning a *How to Make a New City Your Own* blog before she shook her head and returned to reality. She would just be exposing herself, giving away her new location and potentially putting not only herself at risk again, but Maia and her husband, too.

"No," she said, interrupting Maia's flowery description of the Nashville music scene that could have been made into a tourist brochure. "I'm not letting one hateful person destroy my life, and I'm not bringing these threats to your doorstep. I'll be careful, but I'll deal with this on my own and not put anyone else in danger."

Maia opened her mouth, looking prepared to argue, but Gina's resolution must have shown on her face. Maia visibly sighed. "You'll at least go to the police?"

Gina nodded. "Yes, of course. I'll—"

A shriek of laughter interrupted her, making her already tense body startle before she felt a shudder of relief when she recognized the sound. It was only Tara, her landlord's daughter, playing in the yard. The fleeting and acute sensations of being frightened and then relieved were replaced by a heavy sense of acceptance that Gina felt would never go away. Maia was right—she had to go. If she stayed here, in this home where she had felt more creativity and freedom and happiness than she ever had in her life, then she might be leading her internet abusers directly to Tara and her family. Gina couldn't bear it if anyone so much as threw an egg at the house, let alone hurt any of the people inside it. This might be her fight, but she wouldn't be so selfish as to put anyone else in danger.

"Oh, honey, I'm so sorry," Maia said, apparently able to read the expressions on Gina's face as she experienced each one in turn. "What are you going to do?"

Gina's mind was accustomed to making plans, and it took over even now, when most of her wanted to curl up and hide from the world. Now, though, instead of planning exciting outings for her blog posts or a way she could convert her daily projects into viral how-to videos, she was organizing her escape. Her way out of the life in which she desperately wanted to stay.

"Talk to the Andersons first," she said, ticking the boxes on her mental checklist and starting with the family who had opened their home to her. "Then the police."

Then what? Gina sat on the phone for another hour with Maia, going over her options and formulating a graceless exit from her comfortable world. She'd have to revisit every social media site and platform yet again, leaving posts that made it clear she had moved out of her home and city. Her departure had to be as public as possible, but her destination couldn't be. She'd make arrangements to move her belongings into storage and herself into a cheap hotel until she could find an interim place to live—somewhere out of the way and private that she could use as a temporary base until she felt ready to establish herself somewhere permanent again.

Part of Gina's calculations included her meager savings account. She'd have to get her sites going again as soon as possible because she couldn't afford to live any other way. She couldn't go far from this city, where she had sponsors and connections she had worked so hard to develop because she relied on them for a lot of her income. The only thing she knew with certainty as her world crumbled around her was that she was never going back to her old home in eastern Washington or anyplace like it, no matter what.

Chapter Two

A chorus of songbirds serenaded Wren Lindley as she tackled her morning chores. Only a month earlier, she had trundled the morning feed carts from paddock to paddock in the dark, following the gravel paths that were ingrained in her muscle memory as easily as if they were lit by spotlights. Now, even though the early morning air was still chilly enough to require a thick sweater, the late March sun was casting a gray light. Soon it would be high enough in the sky to bring color to Wren's farm, as well as brightness. The washed-out ground of the pastures would become a lush carpet of brilliant emerald grass, and the dark and spiny branches of the apple trees that lined the outdoor arena would reveal the new growth of soft, mint-colored leaves and tightly budded pink and white blossoms.

For this magical hour, though, Wren enjoyed the blurred dullness of the world around her because it made her feel isolated—alone in the quiet of predawn when life was still enough for the chirps of birds and gentle munching of the horses to fill the space. She pushed one cart, which was filled with portioned-out buckets of grain and supplements, and pulled the second—saving herself an extra trip—that was piled high with flakes of hay. Low nickers greeted her as she approached each pen, and contented crunching followed her after she doled out the feed and moved on to the next horse. Her two dogs gamboled along the path ahead of her, the new beagle puppy trying valiantly to keep up with the taller, more agile Great Pyrenees as he flitted, ghostlike, through the shadows.

By the time Wren got back to the barn with her empty carts, the day had brightened considerably. The sky overhead was blue and clear, but Wren could read the low-lying clouds over Liberty Bay well enough to expect rain by afternoon. She figured the sunny weather would last long enough for her to ride—three training horses, plus her own gelding—and teach the single lesson she had on the day's schedule. She fed the dogs and cleaned stalls while the horses finished eating and digesting their breakfasts, and then she brought her horse Sea Foam into the grooming stall.

She took her time getting ready, brushing mud and dust from the gray horse's coat until the near-perfect circles of his dapples were visible again. She brushed his thick tail gently, painstakingly picking out tangles by hand to keep from pulling any hairs loose. He enjoyed rolling in the plentiful spring mud every chance he got, making the task of keeping him clean a constant work in progress. Wren didn't mind. If the business of running the stable didn't get in the way, she would happily spend most of her waking hours fussing around her horse.

She wrapped his legs in protective black bandages and then put a clean white pad and her black leather dressage saddle on his back. She buckled on a matching black bridle with a bit she had polished to a bright shine after her last ride. Wren stepped back and checked to make sure everything was in place. Clean, simple, elegant. She smiled as she put on her gloves and helmet. Putting this much effort into her horse's turnout for a routine schooling session might seem like overkill to some riders, but to Wren this ritual of getting ready was as much part of her riding as anything she did while on the horse. Every small step in her routine connected her to the long chain of riders and trainers who had come before her.

Wren climbed on the mounting block and swung into the saddle. If early morning feeding time was her favorite part of the day, then this first moment of contact with the saddle and horse was definitely her second favorite. She walked Foam down a gentle slope and into the arena. Her dogs trailed behind, lying down on the grassy hillside to keep guard while she rode.

The thick tanbark footing muffled the sound of the gelding's hooves as he and Wren walked and trotted around the outdoor arena. A low white railing, only a few inches off the ground, delineated the regulation-sized twenty-by-sixty meter rectangle, and letters were placed at intervals along the four sides. Wren moved her horse from letter to letter, making circles and serpentines until he felt supple and balanced. A slight shift of her weight brought him from a canter to a walk, and she reached forward to pet and praise him as he stretched his neck, dropping his nose low to the ground as he relaxed after the workout. Wren kept her reins long and loose as he cooled out at a walk, but her mind stayed active, analyzing the session and planning tomorrow's ride. Their first competition of the season was coming up soon, and Wren wanted him to be ready for the move up to the Intermediate levels.

The next three horses she rode were far below Foam's level, but Wren put the same amount of effort into grooming and schooling them as she had with her own horse, as if they were about to enter an Olympic-level show ring. They would be competing at the upcoming competition, as well, with two of Wren's junior riders and one of her adult students.

Wren was just finishing her last ride on Jasper when the dogs leaped to their feet and ran toward the parking lot at the front of the barn, the deep barks of Grover, the Pyrenees, accented by the shriller yips of the pursuing beagle. Her horse shied at the sudden noise, and Wren soothed him with a quiet voice, pushing down her own irritation at the interruption. The visitor was most likely Dianna, Wren's friend and the student she was expecting for a lesson, and Wren was always glad to see her. Still, she found the transition jarring as she had to move from the privacy of her morning to the busier, more public, afternoon.

She dismounted and led Jasper into the barn. Dianna had Pixie, her small bay mare, in the crossties and was currying her already shiny coat. Grover was sitting nearby, begging for attention every time she moved past him, while Biscuit was chewing on the plastic handle of a hoof pick.

Wren greeted Dianna and rescued the pick from the beagle as she led her horse past Pixie and to the adjoining grooming area. She shook her head ruefully as she unbuckled the gelding's bridle. "Lucky you. You barely need to groom her. She's as careful to stay clean as Foam is determined to get dirty."

"I know. She's an angel." Dianna grinned but didn't stop brushing. "This is as much for me as it is for her, though. It helps me mentally scrub away stress from work."

"How much stress can you have at the office? You tell me all the time how much you love your job." Wren slipped the bridle over Jasper's ears and replaced it with his halter.

"Usually I do, but lately I've been getting more and more frustrated with one of my most irritating clients. She won't listen to any of my advice and will probably lose her farm because of her stubbornness."

Uh-oh. Wren had apparently walked right into that one. She wasn't sure what she had done, but she knew Dianna didn't have any other clients with farms.

"I understand about challenging clients," she said, draping the saddle and bridle over her arm and turning toward the tack room. "I have one student who can't seem to understand the phrase *Sit up straight* no matter how many different ways I try to say it."

She rounded her shoulders and walked down the barn aisle with an exaggerated slouch.

"I think that says more about your lack of teaching skills than your poor client's abilities," Dianna called after her, in what might have been an indignant tone if she hadn't been laughing as she spoke. Her notoriously poor posture had been the topic of many of their lessons. She hunched in the saddle the same way she hunched over her desk when she was working on accounts. "Maybe a thesaurus would help you find a more effective way to communicate what you mean."

Wren put away her tack and came back into the barn aisle. "I really don't believe that my vocabulary is the problem," she said. She smiled, hoping her change in subject would be distracting enough to keep Dianna focused on riding and not on lecturing Wren about finances. Wren was willing to do whatever it took to keep her small stable alive, but she hated the idea of trading quality training and teaching for quantitative success. She was perfectly content with the balance she had struck between running a part-time business that gave her plenty of time to enjoy the privacy of her farm. Unfortunately, most of Dianna's plans involved having more people invade Wren's home. Wren did her best to avoid all *You need more clients* lectures. "I have a few exercises we can try today. Remember, it's not just about looking pretty on the horse. If your back is stiff, your horse's spine will be stiff, too."

"Yes, Teacher," Dianna said, giving Pixie one last swipe with a finishing brush, and then setting her bucket of brushes aside. "I will endeavor to be supple and graceful in the saddle.

And after my lesson we'll return to the discussion about money, and you'll endeavor to—"

"To ignore you?" Wren asked hopefully.

Dianna shook her head. "To be open-minded and willing to change."

Wren clipped Jasper's lead rope to his halter and led him across the aisle to his stall. She frowned as if considering the possibility. "Oh, I doubt it. That doesn't really sound like me."

"And I'm not tall and willowy with the posture of a queen." Dianna pulled on a pair of riding gloves and led Pixie toward the arena. Wren and the dogs walked alongside her. "Maybe we can rub off on each other. You can become more reasonable, and I'll look less like a sack of potatoes in the saddle."

Wren wasn't convinced, but she had to admit that Dianna made more of an attempt to change than she did. As soon as she was mounted on Pixie, she focused only on Wren's instructions and not on Wren's shortcomings as a business owner. Wren coaxed her along in her riding, never pushing too hard for grand results while always aiming for the comfort and safety of both Dianna and Pixie. Wren's personal riding ambitions might encompass the never-ending, never truly possible search for perfection that seemed to define the sport of dressage, but Dianna had less lofty—although equally valid and important—goals. She rode for pleasure and for the thrill of learning something new, for physical exercise and a mental break from her real life.

Although Wren loved challenging herself and her horses in competitions, she understood Dianna's approach to riding, too. Especially on days like this one, with enough sun to warm them and enough cloud cover to keep the glare and heat under control. Wren's property had a tiered effect, with the barn and paddocks on the uppermost level, and the arena situated on a slightly lower ledge. Beyond the riding ring, a grass and brush covered hillside sloped more steeply toward the pebbly beach of Liberty Bay. The colorful marina and busy waterfront shops of Poulsbo were just visible to the northeast, across the bay, but the land on Wren's side of the bay was sparsely dotted with homes and farms. Most days, the only traffic she heard was the occasional boat. The waterway was busier in the summer months, but the buffer of green space gave her farm a private feel. She could understand why someone like Dianna would enjoy coming out here to ride and to find a peaceful escape from more urban life. But if too many people came here to get away from the bustle of city life, all they'd end up doing would be to bring that bustle and crowded feel to Wren's farm.

Wren was hopeful that she had distracted Dianna enough to keep her from returning to the subject of finances. During the lesson, Dianna seemed wholly absorbed in listening to Wren's directions and attempting to follow them. After the ride, while Wren helped her groom Pixie and clean her tack, Dianna remained focused on the subject of dressage, asking questions about training and dissecting her performance during the lesson. After Dianna had put away her tack and snapped her locker shut, Wren started edging toward the door, ready to shoo Dianna on her way.

"Nope," Dianna said. She pointed at one of the large wooden tack trunks that lined the walls of the tack room. "Sit."

Wren was about to make a big show of her reluctance, complete with eye rolls and dramatic sighs, but she figured theatrics wouldn't dissuade Dianna from this talk. She sat down, crossing her arms over her chest, and Dianna perched on a small stepladder across from her.

"Property taxes are going up," she said, switching her laser focus from riding to money in an instant. "So is the price of hay. Not to mention the fees for all the shows you're planning to ride in this season. And what did I see in the front pasture when I got here?"

Damn. Wren had thought she was being sneaky putting the gelding as far from the barn as possible. "In the pasture? Probably a horse. I thought we learned how to identify those in your first lesson."

"Funny. By horse, do you mean a new boarder whose owner is prepared to pay—in cash, not in trade—for lessons and training? Or do you mean a money-guzzling freeloader that you couldn't resist buying for yourself?"

"Ouch," Wren said, surprised by the stern tone in Dianna's usually cheery voice. She'd pretty much wrapped up Wren's misguided approach to finances in a single sentence, but still...ouch. "He'll be offended if he hears you calling him names like *freeloader*. He's fully prepared to pay his way by providing hours of joy in exchange for a small amount of grain each day."

"Are you planning to have the county tax assessor come out here and trot around on him for an hour or two instead of getting paid?"

"No, but I *will* let you ride him." Wren tried to make the suggestion sound as tempting as if she was offering a ride on a Grand Prix champion instead of a mixed breed she'd just rescued. "But only if you stop talking about money."

"I'll stop talking about it once you start earning more of it," Dianna said, crossing her arms and mirroring Wren's stubborn posture. "Unless, of course, you have some successful investments you're keeping from me. Or a mattress full of cash? More than twenty dollars in your wallet?"

Wren squinted, mentally counting the cash she had on hand. Probably closer to four dollars than twenty since she had stopped by the feed store yesterday afternoon. She wanted to argue more, but Dianna was right about the skyrocketing prices of feed. She would never skimp on quality for her animals, but even switching to an all-ramen diet for herself wouldn't cover her monthly feed bills. "Fine. I'll try to get one new client in exchange for the new horse."

Dianna shook her head. "You have at least ten empty stalls. Fill them. With people who will pay each month and not take advantage of your generosity by offering to trade burritos for lessons."

"One time," Wren said indignantly. "I only did that once. And it was tamales. Besides, you're one to talk. Should I turn down your accounting services and ask you to pay a board bill?"

Wren really hoped Dianna wouldn't call her bluff. She had been fighting Dianna's advice for months now, conceding on small points and only making minor changes to her business, but now the seriousness and concern she saw in her friend's expression sent a frisson of worry through her. She might have dug herself into a deeper hole than she had realized, and she wasn't delusional enough to believe she could get herself out on her own.

Dianna apparently didn't have much faith in her abilities, either. She shook her head at Wren's suggestion. "Don't be ridiculous. Trading lessons for my help is probably the only fiscally intelligent decision you've made in your life. And it was my idea in the first place."

"Those chronically hunched shoulders of yours must make it easier to pat yourself on the back," Wren muttered.

"My shoulders are hunched because I'm being crushed by concern over your farm's future. It's time for you to share the burden."

Wren winced at the guilt Dianna's words induced in her. She needed Dianna's help, but she was the one ultimately responsible for her farm. She had to stop pretending such crass things as mortgage payments and debt didn't exist in her perfect world of peace and quiet and horses.

"Okay, I'll do it. Finding a few clients shouldn't be hard. I'll let the farrier and vet know I have some space, and maybe after the show season I can take on one new one at a time—"

Dianna held up her hand. "You're thinking slow and old-school. Word of mouth is fine if you have months of leisure during which to build a client base. But you don't. We need to build your business at the speed of—"

"Don't say it," Wren warned her.

"—the internet," Dianna finished, ignoring Wren's plea.

"I don't have a computer," Wren reminded her.

"Then find someone who does. Someone who can help you develop your brand and market yourself properly. You're one of the top riders in the state, but you only have a handful of low-level clients who pay low-level prices. If you were smarter about advertising yourself, you could end up making more money with fewer clients."

Wren liked the sound of those last few words, even though the rest of Dianna's suggestion made her feel distinctly uncomfortable.

"I'm guessing this will be expensive," Wren said. How many extra clients would she need to take on just to cover the overpriced fees of some internet hack?

Dianna shrugged. "Trade for it. Board, lessons, whatever. You're bound to have something someone wants."

Wren looked out the window to her right, but all she could see were the tops of fir trees. Her place was simple, offline, mostly off the grid. She had nothing here that someone with that kind of computer savvy could possibly want.

Chapter Three

The office phone rang just as Wren was clipping one of the crosstie ropes to Foam's halter. She growled in annoyance and snapped the second rope in place before jogging down the aisle. She grabbed the receiver off the wall.

"What?" she barked. She hated phones. The only reason she had conceded to having one in the barn was because she needed to be able to call the vet if one of her horses was sick or hurt, but she seemed to spend most of her time on it fielding unsolicited sales calls. For someone who rarely gave out her number, she was surprisingly popular with a wide range of diet pill and credit card companies.

"Lindley Training Stables, where future Olympians begin the journey to success," Dianna responded in a lilting voice.

"I am not saying that every time I answer the phone."

"Can we compromise on having you say hello like a normal, reasonably friendly person?"

"I can say good-bye like a reasonably busy person. Will that work?"

Dianna laughed. "I take it your interview didn't go well this morning?"

Wren perched on the edge of her worn wooden desk and propped her booted feet on the chair, swiveling it back and forth as she spoke. "She didn't show up. Which actually makes her the front-runner so far, given the rest of the applicants."

"Have they really been that bad, or are you just being grumpy?"

Wren smiled. It was a logical question given how vocal she'd been about her reluctance to hire a social media marketer for her barn. The interviews had been awkward to say the least, especially since the online world had changed drastically since Wren had last been exposed to her family's discussions about it, and now she had to rely on the list of questions and buzzwords Dianna had given her. Maybe she'd sound less ridiculous saying them if she had bothered to memorize them instead of reading directly off the list, but she hadn't found the time.

"Surprisingly enough, I don't think my personality is to blame this time. The first interviewee yesterday wasn't old enough to drive, so her mother brought her. The girl kept asking how fast my horses could gallop and if they knew any tricks. *Tricks*," Wren repeated, in case Dianna hadn't realized how grievous the issue was. "And the second interview was with a guy who apparently thought dressage was some kind of martial art. We talked for half an hour before we realized we were carrying on two separate conversations."

"Well, you've told me that the modern sport of dressage has roots in military training. That's sort of the same thing."

"Not really, no." Wren sighed. Of course Dianna would throw one of Wren's routine lectures about the origins of dressage back at her. The interview had left her frustrated because the guy had seemed qualified and nice enough for Wren to begin to reconcile herself to hiring him. Once they straightened out their miscommunication, and he told her his regular fees, she had to decline. Which just meant more awful interviews in her future. "Anyway, Ms. No Show is looking like the candidate to beat so far. I really liked the fact that she wasn't here."

"Yes, I can see how that would appeal to you. We'll keep her in mind in case we can't find anyone who will actually show up and do the work. Oh, and I have someone stopping by later today. She just called this morning and seems really nice."

Wren's feet slipped off the chair and sent it rolling across the office. The only thing worse than anticipating interviews was having them sprung on her with no notice. She wasn't even sure where she'd put the list of Dianna's questions. Probably in the trash. "I'm sure she's a delight, but can you reschedule for some other day? I was just about to ride Foam, and then I need to go to the grocery store and...Hey, I hear a car."

"That'll be her. Gotta go." Dianna hung up before Wren could get another word in, for all the good it would have done her. She heard Grover's deep woofs coming from the parking area in front of the barn. The least she could do was rescue the visitor from the furry welcoming committee. Or could she hide under the desk until she went away? Wren considered that option for several seconds before she pulled herself to her feet and headed outside.

The car in the parking lot was a nondescript tan hybrid. Grover was peering in the window, at eye level with the driver and blocking her from Wren's view.

"You can get out," she called, whistling to call Grover to her. Biscuit ignored her, as usual, but he was small enough not to be threatening.

"You're sure it's safe?"

The woman who climbed out of the car was anything but nondescript. She was nearly as tall as Wren's five foot eight inches, but curvy and beautiful while Wren was all angles and lines. Her hair was interesting, shading from dark brown to a sort of reddish color, and then lighter blond at the ends. Wren curled her hands into fists to keep from imagining running her fingers through the different colors while those large, soft curls wound around her wrists. When had she ever found hair *interesting*, let alone noticed how the auburn tones could make light blue eyes sparkle like cut glass? Unless it was a horse show day, the most she ever did with her own hair was shove it into a haphazard ponytail or cut off chunks when it got in her eyes. The woman smiled as she spoke and bent down to pet the little beagle, so she didn't seem seriously concerned about her safety, but Wren realized she had let far too many seconds pass between the question and her response. She mentally chided herself to quit staring and start speaking.

"It should be. Safe, I mean." Good. Stumbling over her words. *That* was sexy. She cleared her throat and concentrated on speaking in complete sentences. "Biscuit likes to eat shoes, but he usually waits until there aren't any feet in them."

"Good to know. I usually take my shoes off during interviews, but I'll make an exception today." She stood up and made fleeting eye contact with Wren before turning her attention to Grover. "I suppose that one eats cars? Thank goodness he seems to wait until there aren't any people in them. I'm Gina, by the way. Gina Strickland."

Grover walked over to her as if she had been introducing herself to him. "He's Grover. And I'm Wren Lindley."

"Like the bird? What a pretty name. And unusual."

Gina looked up from petting Grover long enough to flash a brilliant smile in Wren's direction. Wren put her hand on her chest, fairly certain she was having some sort of cardiac event. She was going to have to talk to Dianna about sending someone this gorgeous to her farm without fair warning. Wren hadn't minded sounding like a fool as she muddled through her previous interviews. She was, after all, looking for someone who was an expert in social media, so she didn't have to figure it out herself. She felt considerably more reluctant to show Gina the depth of her ignorance in the world of computers. Where was that damned list of questions?

"Um, thanks," Wren said, not bothering to correct Gina on the origin of her name. She never did. She heard Foam's hoof thudding on the mat in the grooming stall. She'd left him standing there alone too long. "Come on inside," she said, gesturing toward the barn aisle. "I just need to put my horse in his stall, and then we can start the interview."

Which Gina would fail, unfortunately. Wren felt bad about it for several reasons. First, Gina seemed like a much more promising candidate than any of the others by far. First, she had actually shown up. Second, she was old enough to drive herself to job interviews. Third, she was carrying a black leather folio that looked a damned sight more professional than martial arts guy's plastic grocery bag or the little girl's Dora the Explorer backpack.

Wren put Foam in his stall with a flake of hay to munch on until she finished talking to Gina. A few questions, some attempts to nod as if she understood the answers, and then Wren would send Gina on her way. She was far too distracting to have hanging about the barn, talking about the internet and taking lessons from Wren. Plus, she was making Wren wish she had something intelligent and insightful to add to a conversation about social media—a topic she had absolutely zero interest in pursuing. She was happy with her decision about how to live her unplugged, offline life, and she didn't want some goddess lounging around her barn making her feel self-conscious or making her question her values. If this interview was for a date, Gina would already have the job.

They wouldn't have much to talk about, but who cared? A little small talk about the weather and the wine, a nice meal, some really hot sex...

Wren sighed. That wasn't what Gina was looking for here. She wanted a job, not a date. Riding lessons or board, not a one-night stand.

She led Gina into the office and shut the door so the dogs wouldn't crowd them in the small space. She had to edge around Gina twice as she retrieved the desk chair from the corner where it had been flung earlier, then searched for the dusty folding chair that had been tucked behind a case of trophies ages ago. Wren could smell cinnamon and honey every time she got too close to Gina—warm scents that should clash with the fresher, outdoorsy aromas of horses and woods but were instead oddly complementary. Plus, they made Wren long to lean close to Gina's neck and inhale. She managed to resist, but barely. She was new to this interviewing process, but she was pretty sure that nuzzling was not encouraged.

She tried to wipe the grime off the folding chair with the long sleeve of her shirt, but she only managed to smear it, not clean it. Gina was dressed casually but suitably for a business meeting in black pants and a lilac pinstriped shirt while Wren was wearing the same jodhpurs she'd had on while feeding, cleaning stalls, and riding two horses. She shrugged and sat down in the chair, crossing her legs and gesturing for Gina to take the reasonably clean one.

Gina took two rapid steps back, bumping into the desk chair and sending it rolling into the wall with a bang. "Oh, sorry. I don't want to take your chair. I can sit in that one."

Wren frowned, escaping her uncomfortable awareness of her attraction to Gina long enough to realize that Gina seemed flustered, too. Wren supposed it made sense for her to be nervous, since she was the one interviewing for the job.

Wren tried to put aside her frustration with this whole project and with her unexpected response to Gina and instead focus on putting her more at ease. After all, she wasn't going to get the job. Wren might as well make the experience brief and painless. "Please, sit. I'm already dirty, anyway. Careful with that one, though. It moves."

Gina pulled the chair closer and sat down. "Yeah, thanks. The little wheels should have been a clue."

She sat perched on the edge of the chair as if ready to bolt, probably because her potential employer had spent more time gazing at her than asking questions. Wren sifted through some possible things to say before she thought of a good opening line. "So, um, why don't you describe your social media experience."

Wren was congratulating herself on coming up with a statement that bought her time to come up with some clever, insightful questions when she realized Gina was looking for a clear space where she could spread out her folio.

"Let me just move some of this…" Wren stood up and made room on the cluttered desk by stacking a bunch of loose invoices and prize lists, and shoving two halters and a pile of jangly metal bits off to one side.

"Thank you," Gina said, putting her folio on the desk and avoiding Wren's eyes again.

"You're welcome, but I'm deducting interview points because you're laughing at my housekeeping skills."

"No, I wasn't," Gina protested, even though the laughter she had been poorly concealing broke free at Wren's words. She waved a hand vaguely at Wren. "I was laughing at your… well, you have a lot of dirt on your pants from the chair."

Wren twisted around and saw the layer of dusty gray coating the seat of her olive green breeches. She'd have to change before she sat in her nice, clean saddle. And she was giving Gina back those lost points and then some, for checking out her backside. She sat down again and pointed at the folio.

"Go on, then. And you'd better impress me. You've got some ground to make up, and we've barely started."

Gina chuckled as she flipped to the first laminated page, either because she was too confident about her qualifications to be worried about slipping out of cool professionalism, or because she found the situation too amusing to care. After about two minutes, Wren realized the first was the most likely. Gina moved through her presentation with ease, moving swiftly through a skimpy and general biography—raised in a small town, moved to a city—and slowing down when she got to the pages filled with screenshots of her online life and numerous graphs detailing her popularity. Most of the phrases about organic growth and affiliates and click-throughs were meaningless to Wren, but a splash of color caught her attention.

"Hey," she said, pointing at Gina's logo, which had a black cityscape silhouette with a cluster of purple peonies in the corner, enclosed in a slender silver oval. "Your clothes match your logo."

"Mostly because it's my favorite color, so I have a lot of clothes in shades of purple," Gina said as she glanced down at her shirt and tugged at the sleeves. "But it's also part of branding myself. If you see anything purple in the next few days, I want you to think of me."

"I probably will," Wren admitted. Or if she smelled cinnamon or looked at her desk chair or closed her eyes and imagined multicolored hair and light blue eyes. She cleared her throat and shifted her attention from Gina to the thought of having to go out and buy an entire computer-coordinated wardrobe. Not. Happening. "I wouldn't have to go around dressed to match a website, would I?"

Gina laughed. "No. But you'd want to figure out what

you'd like future clients to know about who you are and what you do here. Then you choose one or two colors and images that represent that and make sure they're visible to anyone who comes here in person or visits your site."

"Most barns do something similar at horse shows, with matching trunks and blankets and saddle pads." Wren had meant to follow suit once she started competing with her training students, but it hadn't seemed worth the money or effort when she only had one or two horses at each show.

"That's part of what I'd help you do—narrow your focus and send a clear message to your audience. I don't know much about horses, but I know branding, and I can help you define the image you want to project."

"Well, you'll learn plenty about horses during your lessons. If you're hired, of course," Wren said absently. Gina's prospects were looking better, especially if she was going to encourage Wren to buy more horse-related things. She'd have to deal with her attraction somehow, but at the moment most of her brain was now occupied by daydreams about the way her barn aisle could look at horse shows. She still imagined herself with minimal students, but their horses would be decked out in elegant fly sheets and—

"I'm not really interested in the lessons." Gina's voice interrupted Wren's fantasy. "And I don't have a horse to board. Your accountant said you had an apartment to rent in exchange for the work, though, and I need a place to live."

"An apartment? Dianna said you could live here?" Wren frowned as she tried to think of a way to get Gina out of the office for at least a few minutes of privacy. She needed to call her meddling accountant, and she had a feeling the conversation would include more swear words than an interviewee should have to hear.

Gina stood up, as if reading her mind. "She also said I

should excuse myself at this point in the interview and say that I really want to look around the farm, to give you a chance to call her."

Wren waved toward the door. "Fine. Look around. Just don't get too comfortable because you're not moving in." She added the last sentence loudly as Gina shut the office door behind her. She heard her answering laughter, though, and figured Dianna had predicted she would say something along those lines.

"She's not moving in," she said again, as soon as Dianna answered her phone.

"She's very nice. And very well qualified," Dianna said, her voice calm.

"I'm taking away your stirrups for an entire month." Dianna complained incessantly when Wren made her spend even a few minutes in a lesson working on her legs and seat by riding without stirrups. Four weeks without them seemed like a fitting punishment.

"I've checked her out online," Dianna continued, ignoring Wren's threat. "She's an influencer, Wren. High numbers, a brilliantly creative mind, and a real gift for visual storytelling. Combine her skills with your riding talent, and you'll have so many people wanting to train with you that you'll have to turn most of them away. I know how much you'll enjoy that."

Wren rolled her eyes. "I don't enjoy turning people away. I just don't want too many of them coming here in the first place."

She flipped through Gina's folio as she talked, finding an outlet for some of her irritation as she snapped through the pages.

"You can't afford to pay someone of her caliber, let alone bribe them to work in exchange for a few lessons. You can't pass up this opportunity."

Wren snorted. Yes, she could. Quite happily, too. "If she's as amazing as you say, then why would she be swayed by a studio apartment in my barn? You've seen it. There are spiders."

She paused on a page in the folio's section on Gina's Instagram, where she had included photos of her Seattle apartment. It was a bright-looking space, with lots of color and texture. Even someone as design-challenged as Wren could see that this would be a beautiful place to live. Eclectic—but in a carefully crafted and thoughtful way. Not in the whatever-the-hell-I-can-find way Wren had decorated her own home.

"She needs a place to stay for a while, Wren."

Something in Dianna's tone of voice made Wren stop and close the binder. "What happened to her?"

"Ask her. It's her story to tell. But just…she needs a place, and you really could use her help."

"Two months. No stirrups," Wren said before she hung up the phone.

Chapter Four

Gina stepped out of the office and was bombarded by Wren's dogs. The one called Grover was intimidatingly huge, but he merely wanted to lean against her legs. The littler Biscuit, adorable as he was with his floppy ears and patchy brown and black spots, was apparently the vicious one of the pair. He launched himself at the hem of her pants and grabbed hold with determined teeth. Gina reached down and detached him, careful not to shred any fabric. She didn't actively dislike dogs, but she had never spent much time around them. Her dad had owned hunting dogs when she was growing up, though they were meant to be working animals and were off-limits as pets. She had gotten in trouble the few times she had tried to befriend them by bringing table scraps or teaching them tricks, so she had quickly learned to avoid the kennels. She was a sucker for dog videos on YouTube when she had trouble sleeping at night, with their montages of animals welcoming their owners home from war or big dogs cuddling tiny kittens, but her canine encounters were restricted to online ones— never in person. These two, with their complete disregard for personal space, were just another reminder of how far this place was pushing her outside of her comfort zone.

"Come on, you two," she said with a sigh. "We might as well look around."

She led the dogs down the aisle toward the back door of the barn. The only place she really wanted to look around was the inside of her car as she was driving away, but she had to see this through. She was exhausted after the stress of telling her awful story over and over when all she wanted to do was forget about it. She'd explained the situation to her landlords, apologizing for bringing this mess directly to their doorstep. They had been sympathetic and kind, even telling her to contact them again when she was ready to move back to Seattle because they'd let her return if the apartment was still available. Gina had thanked them and said she would, but she could see the worry on their faces and knew she wouldn't ever be coming back to the lovely space she had been turning into a home.

Next had come the lengthy visit to the police department. The officers had been kind, but she'd had to repeat the graphic details of the doxing three times as she was shuffled from person to person before she finally got to someone who was able to help her. Not that their help was anything as satisfying as catching the cruel people who had posted her personal information, and giving her the freedom to return to her normal life. No, their help was more along the lines of thanking her for giving them the information, promising to look into the matter, and suggesting she find someplace safe to stay for a while. Someplace out of the way, where she couldn't be traced.

Gina paused by one of the stalls and patted the nose of a gray horse that was looking at her with enormous brown eyes. This farm was as out of the way as she was prepared to go. She had pored over a map of the state, searching for isolated pockets that would still give her driving access to Seattle and other interesting places she could blog about while keeping her living situation a secret. Poulsbo hadn't been at the top of her list—or anywhere on it—since she hadn't wanted to leave the I-5 corridor and head out to the Olympic Peninsula, but she had spotted the ad that Dianna had presumably posted for Wren when she was scrolling through local classifieds in search of an apartment that wouldn't cost a fortune. She had called on a whim, and as soon as she found out that the job might come with a place to live, she had decided to give it a shot no matter how undesirable the location. She would have spent more energy regretting that decision if she thought there was any chance in hell that Wren would concede to having her move onto her property. Neither one of them wanted Gina to be here.

Even if Wren decided for some reason to offer her the job, Gina would then be forced to tell her why she desperately and immediately needed a place like this to live, where she couldn't be easily traced, but also where she could continue to run her business. She'd be sent packing for sure once Wren understood the potential risk caused by Gina's presence. She was tempted to keep her secret from a potential new employer, but her conscience wouldn't allow her to move in without being honest about her situation. How many more times would she be forced to rehash those damned comments before she would be able to settle into some new version of normal?

Gina jumped back as the gray horse snorted at her, breaking her out of her ruminations. She continued walking down the aisle, staying in the center and as far away from the horses on either side as she could be. She'd just have to suck it up and repeat the story as many times as necessary. The hardest recounting had been the vaguest, oddly enough. She had posted an abbreviated version of the hateful virtual attack on every platform she used, assuring her followers that she would continue to post and repeatedly proclaiming that she had moved from her old location and that the police were involved—doing her damnedest to keep anyone from harassing her landlords or their family. She had also apologized to her viewers for switching to a mediated format and not allowing everyone to post freely as they had before. She had been overwhelmed by the immediate outpouring of kindness from her online communities, as her friends and followers expressed their shock at what had happened, as well as their wishes for her to find a safe place. And she answered every single one. She had long since stopped replying to every one of the thousands of comments left on her various channels. She read them, of course, and answered similar questions with single replies, but she didn't have enough hours in the day to compose thousands of replies. Now she had to find those hours, as well as the ones required for her to review and accept each comment before it was made public.

Gina made it to the end of the barn aisle, stepping outside and looking around. The day was cool, but the cloud cover was wispy enough to let plenty of sunshine through to spotlight the farm's attributes. Large paddocks to her right, the bright green of the spring grass contrasting nicely with the grazing horses in various shades of brown and gray. A riding arena with red-brown footing and a low white rail marking its borders. Tall evergreens fringing the property, their highest branches swaying slightly in a breeze she was unable to feel at ground level. And the crown jewel of the view—the sparkling water of one of Puget Sound's many inlets.

Nature. Yep, just the way it looked when she lived in her childhood home, far from the concrete and glass of the city. She had left this kind of rustic emptiness behind years ago, and she still couldn't believe she might have to return to this type of living situation, even if only for a short time. She was sure plenty of people, like Wren, loved this peaceful, boring, empty kind of life far from the energy and amenities of a big city. They could have it, because Gina sure as hell didn't want it. She already felt out of range of sponsors, slowly slipping off their radar…

She took out her phone and snapped a few photos of Liberty Bay and the arena. Just because she didn't want to live here didn't mean she didn't see the opportunity for capturing some pictures for her Instagram. She was careful not to include anything that might reveal her location, and she hated having to control her photography that way. Still, she flicked through the images quickly, feeling an irritating wave of relief when she saw how generic the glimpses of fir trees and water were. She could have taken the shots pretty much anywhere in western Washington. She had no idea how she would manage to incorporate her personal style of blogging and creating photo stories with her current need to remain hidden.

Gina sensed Wren's presence behind her, even before the dogs shifted their focus in the direction of the barn. Gina slid her phone into her pocket and turned away from the water. Wren was scowling at her, which had to mean Gina had the job. She'd probably be grinning with glee if she was anticipating tossing Gina off her property. Damn it. Gina's best hope for escaping this place had been Wren's obvious desire to avoid any marketing that would threaten her quiet farm.

She had been warned by Dianna about Wren's reluctance to have anyone associated with the internet come onto her property and interrupt her tech-free life, and she apparently hadn't been exaggerating. There was something unexpectedly appealing about Wren's deadpan way of saying grouchy things that made them sound funny rather than rude, though, and Gina felt more at ease with her banter than she would have been with someone who was rigidly polite and less honest.

Actually, there were way too many things about Wren that Gina found appealing. She was elegant, but with absolutely no artifice. Gina knew people who seemed to aspire to Wren's type of presence, using perfect makeup or designer clothes or carefully crafted personalities to make their statements. Wren's charisma was something intangible. Something potent. Not to mention her killer body, shown off to perfection in those tight riding pants and tall leather boots. When she sat down and crossed those sexy legs Gina had…well, she had stumbled into a chair. Not the smoothest move. Somehow, she had managed to keep from drooling all over the desk, especially once she started talking about her passion for her work and could keep most of her focus off Wren and on the interview. And she'd have to continue to fight her body's response to Wren if she expected to live here and work with her. Her life was complicated enough as it was without adding romantic entanglements to the mix. Not that Wren seemed inclined to ask her on a date. She was more likely to have her arrested for trespassing.

"Come on, then. I'll show you the apartment." Wren whistled, and Grover trotted up the slight hill toward her with Biscuit loping behind and Gina following at a less enthusiastic walk.

"Did you just whistle at me like I'm a dog?"

"No. I whistled at the *dogs*, and I *told* you to come on," Wren said. "But who's a good girl for coming when she's called?"

Wren said the last sentence in exaggerated baby talk, and Gina laughed, catching herself as she felt an uncharacteristic urge to playfully shove at Wren's shoulder. She usually felt awkward around people she'd just met—well, around most people in real life, no matter how long she'd known them. She could chat with thousands through the lens of her camera, but she rarely felt the same sense of relaxation and ease in person. For some reason, Wren's company put her at ease, even as her physical presence set Gina's nerve endings at full attention.

Wren led her up a rickety flight of rough wooden stairs set against the outside wall of the barn. Gina figured they were bolted to the building, but they swayed enough as she climbed to make her question her assumption.

"Well, here it is," Wren said, pushing the door open and standing back to let Gina walk through. "Feel free to hate it and turn down the job."

"If the state of this staircase is any indication of the apartment's condition, I'm sure I'll love it," Gina said, stepping past Wren on the small landing and into the room. The warped wood gave a squeak of protest when she moved, as if adding emphasis to her sarcastic comment.

"There's a good chance the floor will give out one of these days, and you'll fall into the stall below you," Wren said, in what sounded suspiciously like a hopeful voice.

"I think that would qualify as an upgrade to my living situation." Gina looked around the apartment, clearly disused for years. The room was small and rectangular, maybe spanning the length of four of the stalls Gina had seen in the barn underneath her. The kitchen was tiny, with a linoleum floor and dated appliances. The rest of the room had a low-pile green carpet, barely a step up in comfort and appearance from laying a thin sheet of fabric on the floor. Every surface was covered with a layer of dirt, and the enclosed space had a musty, bitter smell. The stalls below even with horses in them—smelled better than this place.

But the walls were covered with beautiful, knotty wood panels, and the two large picture windows had a view of the bay below, with Mount Rainier in the distance. Most importantly, the farm was hidden away enough for her to feel safe, which had to be her priority at the moment, until she figured out the best way to move forward and get past this setback. Wren's desire for a private setting would work for Gina. She made a choice to talk about her cyberabuse as little as possible. She'd tell Wren, and if she was willing to have Gina stay, she would. She wasn't going to shop around for apartments or jobs with living arrangements and have to recount the story multiple times. Besides, this place had definite potential for improvement. Well, at least it had little room for getting worse.

"I like it," she said with a nod, her mind already spinning with ideas for a new redecorating blog series. *From Nearly Condemned to Country Chic in Seven Easy Steps* had potential.

"Really?" Wren asked in an incredulous voice. "What's your favorite part? The cobwebs?"

"I won't have to decorate for Halloween. Just think of all the time and money I'll save."

Wren pointed toward the bathroom. "There's a composting toilet."

Gina tried to think of a snappy comeback to that unexpected and disconcerting piece of information, but she couldn't come up with anything. "Ugh. You're not using the compost on a vegetable garden, are you? If so, I'm not coming over for dinner."

"I didn't ask you to. But are you seriously saying you'd rather have vegetables grown in chemical fertilizer?"

"Absolutely," Gina said. She sighed, moving toward one of the windows and looking out but not focusing on anything in particular. "Did Dianna tell you why I need a new place to live?"

"She didn't give me the reason. You can, if you want, but it isn't necessary." Wren's voice softened, as if she sensed that this topic wasn't one Gina was prepared to turn into a joke.

"It really is," Gina answered. She told Wren the whole story, not leaving out any of the details so she would fully understand, but keeping all emotion out of her voice. Part of her wanted to face Wren while she spoke, to try to gauge her reaction and anticipate her rejection. The other part preferred staring out at the trees and mountain that were solid and untouched by her petty human problems.

She made herself turn around when she was finished, half expecting Wren to shove her out the door. Wren's expression was unreadable and mobile, as if she was processing several feelings at once.

"I...that's terrible, and you didn't deserve to have it happen to you."

She paused, and Gina waited for the *but...*

But now you need to leave.

But I don't want someone who might have a crazed stalker living here.

"Do you want to keep Grover with you at night, at least for a few days? He'll protect you and make you feel safe until you get used to being here."

Gina felt a sharp pang of tears at the unexpected kindness. She had been prepared for Wren to tell her to leave, and she had spent the entire afternoon thinking about how much she would hate living so far from the city, but the realization that Wren was going to let her stay nearly made her sag to the ground in relief. She had a place to live, and a job to cover her rent in case she lost sponsors or advertisers. And apparently a temporary dog, if she wanted one. She didn't, of course. Her black pants were already covered with white hairs, and having a dog drooling and shedding in this place certainly wouldn't increase its level of cleanliness.

"Yes, please," she heard herself saying in spite of herself, as if from a distance. She pulled herself together. She'd make this new life work because she needed to return to her old one as soon as possible. She would be stronger for having gone through this and survived. She nodded firmly, as if sealing a promise to herself. She'd get back to the city. Back where she belonged. And next time, she'd be prepared to protect herself.

"Fine." Wren ran a hand through her hair. "So, I have my routines out here, and I'm sure you'll settle into your own. Maybe it's best if our lives intersect as little as possible, unless we're working on advertising or whatever."

She gestured vaguely with the last word, and Gina wondered if Wren had any idea what to do with her new social media expert. No matter. Gina knew enough for both of them.

"You won't even know I'm here," she promised.

CHAPTER FIVE

C an you name the five aids that we use to communicate with our horses?"

"I'm on a rocket ship," Eric shrieked in response. Callie, his small Appaloosa mare, trudged along with barely a flick of her ear at the shrill sound.

Wren sighed. *Lord, give me strength.* Was there a patron saint for people who had to teach *anything* to eight-year-old boys? She needed to find out and start making some serious offerings.

"Do you want to play the name-the-parts-of-the-saddle game?"

"We're going to the moon!" Eric stood up in his stirrups and flung one arm skyward.

Apparently not. Wren closed her eyes briefly. She tried to count to ten but was too distracted by the *vroom* noises Eric was making to get past four.

"Do you want to trot?"

Eric sat down again. "Yes, please," he said in a normal, nonmotorized voice. He knew her well enough by now to understand that she wouldn't let him do anything exciting like trotting if he wasn't quiet and paying attention to her. She needed to work on extending those moments throughout the rest of the lesson, but right now she was just relieved to have these pockets of time when he was well-behaved.

"What do you need to do first?"

"Sit up tall, heels down, and squeeze with my legs. Callie, trot."

The last word was spoken with an upward inflection, and Wren recognized it as a fair imitation of her own voice when she was talking to her horses. In fact, he had pretty much repeated the instructions she had been giving him over the past few weeks word for word. Maybe he really had been paying attention to at least some of the lessons.

She could see he was trying to signal for Callie to trot, but his legs were still too short to reach beyond the leather flaps of the saddle, so Callie couldn't feel when he squeezed her sides. Well, she could probably feel it, but not enough to actually do anything about it. Wren's parents had bought Calypso for her once they realized that their incomprehensible daughter was never going to share their passion for the world of technology, preferring instead to lose herself in the woods and fields surrounding their Northern California home. They had basically handed the little mare to Wren and left her to figure out what to do with her. Calypso had taught Wren how to ride by being an absolute joy when Wren did the right things and dumping her on her ass when she made a mistake. Wren had eventually learned how to make fewer mistakes—by reading horse books, hounding local riding instructors, and mainly through a bruising version of trial and error. Callie was still a great teacher, especially since these days she chose to move as a reward or stop completely as a punishment rather than going through the effort of tossing kids off her back.

As soon as she saw Eric asking the horse to trot correctly—albeit ineffectively—she stepped into the mare's space and made a clucking sound, and Callie eased into a shuffling trot. Wren walked alongside to keep her moving and called out some basic instructions to Eric, which he clearly made an effort to follow with varying degrees of success, given his age and stature.

After a complete circuit of the ring, he was looking winded. "Let's walk," Wren said, as if she had needed to jog to keep up with Callie's slow pace and was as tired as he was. The mare dropped back into her gentle amble probably more because she understood the word *walk* than because Eric's use of the reins was effective.

He leaned forward and patted Callie on the neck. "Give her a pat. She's a good girl," he said.

Wren closed her mouth. She had just been about to say those exact words, using the same tone of voice. It was like teaching a mynah bird.

"You did a great job today, Eric," she said instead. "Why don't you let her walk once around to cool out."

"Can we go Around the World?"

"Sure. Just don't let her stop to eat grass."

"Yay!" Eric steered Callie out of the arena. Around the World was nothing more exciting than the path around the outside of the arena, but Wren's younger students seemed to think it was a daring sort of adventure. They were separated by only the inches-high railing from where they had been riding only minutes before, but the outer path seemed to represent some sort of freedom to them. Wren had a feeling some of her adults felt the same way, although they tended to be less exuberant about it.

Wren watched as Eric started along the track, and then she sighed and flopped onto the grassy hill next to his mother, Linda, who was sitting in a lawn chair and paging through a catalog of riding apparel.

Wren leaned back on her elbows and frowned as an image

of Gina intruded on her mind. She was able to keep thoughts of her slightly at bay while teaching or riding, but as soon as any space opened up in her mind, Gina seemed determined to come along and fill it. Because of what she represented, not because of her as a person. A very beautiful person. With the softest looking hair…

Wren sat up. "He hates these lessons," she said, gesturing toward Eric, who was laughing and chattering away to Callie about the dinosaurs—apparently masquerading as other horses—in the nearby paddocks.

"He loves them," Linda said in a distracted voice. "I need some new riding shirts for the show season. What do you think of light blue?"

"Get white. It's traditional. And he doesn't seem to be having fun."

Linda glanced at her son, who was doing nothing more than walking sedately on Callie, and then she gave Wren an indulgent smile and patted her head. "He's having fun. Just not your idea of fun." She laughed and went back to putting stars next to nontraditional shirts with a red marker. "I'm sure when you were his age you were writing essays debating the merits of classical dressage theories, but your average eight-year-old has less capacity for philosophy than that. He's absorbing everything, and as his attention span and muscles grow, you'll be amazed at how much he's learned from you."

"I didn't write any essays. Just a couple of reports for school."

Linda laughed again. "Besides, I know you don't want to stop teaching him because then who would clean your teeth?"

Wren looked over at Eric, who was flailing around on Callie for no clear reason. "Maybe it wouldn't be so bad if they rotted away," she said, grinning when Linda playfully smacked her with the catalog. Eric was another of Wren's barters, but one for an essential service that Dianna didn't complain about even when she was in one of her accounting moods. Linda paid for her board and lessons, but she'd traded her dental hygienist skills for Eric's lessons when she decided her son was destined to become a dressage rider.

Wren lay back on the grass and stared at the clouds. She always enjoyed trading goods and services like this because it added a different dimension to her business transactions. There was an appreciation of worth and time that seemed to be missing when people handed over cash or plastic in exchange for something they wanted. Instead, she and her clients swapped their own energy and effort.

Wren's idealistic love of bartering was coming back to bite her in the ass now, though. As Dianna said, she couldn't barter for her property taxes, or for a lot of other expenses a farm like this one incurred at an alarming rate. So she needed to make cash.

Enter Gina. Wren sighed. Everything spun back to her now, ever since she had gotten out of her car and smiled at Wren. There had been plenty of opportunities for Wren to tell her to go, but the transition from interview to offering her a place to live had seemed inevitable in some ways, as if Wren really hadn't had a choice. She was the most qualified candidate Wren had seen—even she, with her utter disinterest in social media marketing, could appreciate how far Gina was from the other interviewees in terms of talent and experience. And she was willing to barter for the job, which should have made her the perfect choice for Wren.

Unfortunately, she wanted to trade for the one thing Wren least wanted to give. Her privacy. Having someone around who would not just interrupt the joy of her well-balanced life, but who would completely destroy Wren's peace of mind with scents of cinnamon and curves that were meant to be touched.

She had held on to the belief that she had a choice in the matter until the very end, when Gina told her why she needed to come here, recounting her story that seemed to encapsulate everything Wren disliked and distrusted about the internet in a single episode. The false sense of intimacy when lives were shared online, juxtaposed with how easy it was to be cruel when hiding behind the protection of false names and computer screens. But no matter how fake virtual life could be, the effects of this incident were obviously very real to Gina. Gina had stared out the window while she spoke, her voice calm and detached as she repeated some really horrific words that had been written about her. But Wren had noticed the clues about how Gina was really feeling inside, no matter how hard she tried not to show it. The way she had winced at some of the things she had to repeat, how she had closed her eyes and taken a slow and deep breath before she talked about leaving her apartment behind. And the shine in her eyes when Wren had said Grover could stay with her—close enough to tears that Wren had either had to look away or reach out and hug her.

She had looked away, of course, but the damage had been done, and the choice had been made. Gina would be moving in today, bringing a moving van with all her belongings and no one to help her unload them. She had told Wren she'd manage on her own, and for someone with thousands of followers, she seemed to be sadly lacking in friends.

Not Wren's problem. Gina could take care of herself. And the only reason Wren had spent half the morning cleaning the damned apartment was…well, it just seemed rude not to run a vacuum around the place since it was her fault the room was in such a dirty and disused state. Gina was on her own for the rest, including trying to get a bed or any other furniture up those narrow stairs.

She heard hoofbeats coming up the hill and propped herself on her elbows as Eric and Callie walked over to them. Callie lowered her head to graze as soon as she reached the grassy part of the hill, and Eric let go of his reins so they fell forward draped around Callie's ears. She and Linda gasped in unison, and Wren hurried over to grab the reins before Callie stepped on them. She delivered a lengthy lecture on the dangers of loose horses and broken bridles as they led Callie back to the barn and untacked her, but despite his mom's optimistic assurances, she had serious doubts about how much he was absorbing.

He was useful for keeping her mind off Gina, though. Every time her thoughts would wander, she'd have to pull herself back to the present and stop him from climbing under Callie's belly or hanging from the hook where the riders hung dirty bridles while they cleaned them. He wouldn't always be around to save her from her wandering thoughts, but she doubted she'd need the distraction once Gina was settled here. She'd surely make good on her promise that Wren wouldn't even know she was there, since the barn where Wren spent most of her time was about as unappealing to a techie like Gina as an electronics store would be for Wren. Wren's parents worked in the computer industry, and she knew exactly what to expect from someone like them. Gina would spend her days inside, on her phone or on her computer, with virtual friends and virtually no interest in talking to someone like Wren, who didn't speak her language.

And that was good, because Wren loved her simple life, with no screens to filter out the world around her. Gina seemed anything but simple, and Wren's reaction to her was even less so.

And so she would avoid her. And not care about her or her furniture or anything else.

With significant help from Wren, Eric managed to get Callie groomed and tucked away in her stall, and his saddle and bridle cleaned and hung properly in the tack room. Wren finished putting away Callie's brushes and saddle pad while Linda and Eric went out to the large pasture to visit Linda's horse. She had just shut the locker door when she heard the heavy hay truck pulling into her parking area. She stopped by the office to get her checkbook and went out to meet Nick and his sons.

They had already started backing the truck into position when she arrived in the hay barn, and she waved at Nick as she walked past the cab of the idling truck. The redheaded twins were checking out the old four-wheeler she had parked there earlier in the day. "Oh, sorry. Let me move that."

"I'll do it for you," Mike offered quickly, and she smiled her thanks and tossed him the keys. Liam climbed in with him, and they drove out of the barn. As soon as they were out of the way, Nick finished backing up and got out of the cab.

"Thanks for coming out a few days early," she said, taking the invoice he gave her and filling out a check. "I wasn't sure I'd be around next weekend."

"Not a problem. And if the boys ever manage to find their way back in here, we'll get this lot unloaded for you."

Wren smiled. She could hear the four-wheeler making its second trip around the hay barn. She leaned against one of the support posts and tucked the invoice in her pocket, chatting with Nick about the quality of this year's timothy hay and when he predicted the second cutting would be available. Eventually the twins came back inside, and Mike handed her the keys.

"Thanks," he said, as if she'd done him a favor instead of the other way around. "That was fun."

"Yeah, it's…" Wren paused. How did one compliment a

four-wheeler? She hadn't used the thing since driving it out to the back storage shed a few years ago when a horse show friend had given it to her in exchange for one of Wren's saddles. She had insisted that Wren would never go back to lugging feed carts around again after she got used to a motorized alternative. Wren had managed to avoid that outcome by never using the thing, let alone getting used to it.

"It's a nice little machine," she said, for lack of a better phrase. "I'll probably end up selling it, though, in case you hear of anyone who's interested."

Mike and Liam elbowed each other in a very unsubtle way until Liam finally asked how much she wanted for it.

Nick gave a snort of laughter. "Wrong question, son," he said. "You should be asking *what* she wants for it, not how much."

Wren laughed. Nick knew her better than she thought. "I have a friend coming over tonight. She's going to be staying in the barn apartment until she finds a more permanent place, and we could use some help getting her moved in." She held up her hand before the boys could agree. "Second floor, rickety staircase. And I have no idea how heavy her furniture is. She might be bringing a grand piano or a marble-topped dining room table."

Gina wasn't exactly a friend, but Wren decided it was the easiest story to tell. Dianna knew why she was coming, but no one else needed to. A friend coming to stay meant no lease was needed. No paper trail would lead anyone to Gina.

The boys exchanged pleading looks with their dad, and he nodded. "Seems the boys are getting the better end of the deal, though," he said. "You sure about this?"

"Absolutely," Wren said. She'd much rather have people she trusted helping Gina move, rather than bringing in strangers. She and Gina might have been able to carry her stuff upstairs, but that would mean more time with just the two of them together than Wren was ready to handle. She'd have to manage eventually, if they were going to work together, but for now avoidance was more appealing.

"All right, then. You boys get this hay unloaded. I'll see what I can do about reinforcing that staircase."

The twins high-fived each other and climbed onto the truck while Nick climbed back into the cab to get his tools.

Wren smiled with relief. *Now* she could stop caring about Gina and her furniture and everything else, and go back to living her life like before.

CHAPTER SIX

By the time Gina pulled the moving van into the parking area in front of Wren's barn, she was exhausted and tempted to drive the damned thing into the bay. Minimalist blogs were all the rage right now, anyway. She wasn't sure how many Instagram photos she could post of an empty apartment, but she'd give it a try.

She put the van in park and rested her forehead on the steering wheel. She hadn't thought through the moving portion of this awful new adventure she was on. Her main concern had been keeping a low profile, so she had decided to move herself. She wouldn't have to give anyone this address, and she'd save a ton of money.

Brilliant. Unfortunately, she had conveniently ignored the parts of the scenario in which she had to transport her stuff from the storage locker—where her old landlord had kindly moved it for her—up the ramp into the van. She had spent all day wrestling with each box and piece of furniture, shoving things along inch by inch at times. Writing blog posts and taking photos of desks apparently wasn't sufficient exercise to build upper-body strength. Not to mention the unwieldy items that were just too difficult for one pair of arms to move.

Now she was faced with a steep set of stairs. Plus, her car was still parked at her hotel. She had gone back over the plan she had devised for moving, and nowhere in it had she made arrangements for getting from the rental garage to the hotel. She had been delusional enough to believe she could single-handedly move an entire apartment full of belongings and drive two vehicles at once. She sighed and sat up again. Getting an Uber to take her to her car would be the simplest part of the day. Getting up the energy to come back here and not just live in the hotel until she ran out of money was the hardest—more difficult even than moving her bed up the stairs.

Well, the best she could do was wrestle the mattress up there. She'd have to give in and hire someone to help her with the rest tomorrow. She jumped out of the van and looked around the farm. The sky to her right was tinged with sunset pink, and about a million birds were chirping from their hiding spots in the trees. Nature again. Charming.

Gina put her hands on her lower back and arched her spine, trying to undo some of the kinks from her drive. In another fantastic tactical move, she had found herself on the freeway during the afternoon's heaviest traffic. She hadn't been brave enough to drive the van onto the ferry, so she had taken the long way south to Tacoma, over the Narrows Bridge, and north again to Poulsbo. Along with what seemed to be the state's entire population.

"I hate to interrupt your sunset yoga session, but we should unload this thing before it gets dark."

Gina spun around and nearly crashed into Wren, who had suddenly appeared behind her.

"Where did you come from? Jeez, you could give a person a heart attack sneaking up like that."

Wren scuffed her boot on the pebbly ground. "I was walking on gravel. Who sneaks on gravel? It's loud."

"Well, I couldn't hear you over all this bird noise. Is there something wrong with them?"

Wren gave a kind of half laugh, half frown, as if she was encountering a perplexing alien life-form and trying to figure it out. Gina had seen the same expression on Wren's face several times during her interview. She had a feeling she would see it often—probably every time they interacted.

Gina realized she was still standing overly close to Wren, and she took a step back. Now that she had gotten over her initial surprise, she couldn't understand how she had missed the signs of Wren's presence. Even in the midst of this country setting, Wren's outdoorsy, clean scent somehow overshadowed nature itself. And she had an energy about her that Gina could feel in almost tangible waves. A coiled tension that made Gina feel as if something exciting was about to happen.

She wrapped her arms around her middle and took another step back, bumping into the side of the van. Wren reached out to steady her, putting a hand on her arm as if by reflex but pulling it away again just as quickly.

"Hey, I'm sorry if I startled you. I really did think you heard me coming."

Gina waved off the apology. She was more upset by her body's response to being close to Wren than by the initial scare, but she wasn't about to admit it to Wren.

"It's okay. I'm just a little jumpy these days."

"Understandable." She gestured to Gina's left with her head. "Oh, and Nick is coming up behind you, just to give you a heads-up."

Gina turned in the direction Wren had indicated and saw a balding redheaded man walking toward her. Once she was looking at him, she noticed the sound of his heavy footsteps, but she hadn't registered his approach before Wren's comment. "What are you people?" she asked. "Cat burglars?"

Wren laughed. "It's you, not us. You live in a city. You probably tune out a lot of noise, just out of habit and self-preservation. Give yourself a few weeks here, where there aren't as many sights and sounds competing for your attention, and you'll start to notice the little things again."

"Ah, yes. The joys of the simple life." Gina made a gagging noise.

"I doubt life around you would ever be simple, whether you're in a city or in the middle of nowhere."

Gina tried to read Wren's expression, but the deepening shade of dusk made it hard to even delineate her elegant features, let alone interpret them. The comment hadn't sounded like a compliment, given Wren's obvious distaste for anything that messed up her ordered life, but something in her tone made the words sound almost warm. Gina didn't have a chance to ask her to explain what she meant because Nick got close enough to introduce himself.

"I'll back the van over there, if you want. The boys are waiting for us."

"Oh, thank you. I'd appreciate it," Gina said, handing him the keys. She rarely drove in Seattle, preferring public transportation to the hassles of parking and battling traffic. She figured that would be another skill she'd develop living out here in the boonies. She'd probably be flying around on a tractor like an old pro in a month's time.

"Wait," she said, once she shook the image of herself on a tractor in a flannel shirt and overalls out of her weary mind. "The boys?"

"My sons. Wren asked—"

"I asked them to bring my hay delivery today," Wren interrupted. "And they offered to stick around and carry your furniture up to the apartment. They're nice people."

"Yeah, we're the nice ones." Nick chuckled and shook his head at Wren before opening the van door and climbing in.

"I thought you'd be here sooner," Wren said. "You missed pizza."

She turned away and walked after the van. Gina hesitated a moment before following. Being around one person she barely knew was challenging enough, especially when said person was someone who made her heat up from the inside out whenever she smiled. Spending time in close quarters with three additional strangers was overwhelming. If circumstances were different, she would push through her awkwardness without another thought, like she had done when she met the owners of her old apartment for the first time, but she had wanted to live there. Right now she was putting herself in an uncomfortable position just so she could move into a place where she didn't want to be. She was tempted to cut her losses and run. She could always get new stuff once she found a place to live, right?

If she hadn't left her cell in the van, she might have just vanished into the night, leaving Wren behind sighing in relief because her barn would remain internet-free. Gina smiled to herself at the thought of Wren celebrating the continued vacancy and unwired state of her bug-ridden apartment. She had probably hung the cobwebs in there on purpose, just to keep from tempting any potential tenants.

Most of her curmudgeon act had to be a sham, though, because here she was, unhooking the clasp on the van's rear door as if she was planning to help tote Gina's belongings into the apartment. Gina had expected Wren to stay inside her house, leaving her on her own tonight. Instead, she had even brought reinforcements in the form of two stocky teenage boys and their friendly dad.

"Oh my God, this thing is full. Just how long are you expecting to stay?" Wren asked, peering into the dark van. She pulled out the ramp and lowered it to the ground, shaking her head the whole time.

"For *years*, at least," Gina said, although she had no such intentions. She spread her arms wide and inhaled deeply, releasing her breath with an exaggerated *aaaah* sound. "Maybe forever, since the aroma of horse manure is so intoxicating."

All she really could smell was the slightly fishy scent of the bay and the sweetness of pine, but she wasn't going to admit how pleasant they were, even to herself. The boys snickered at her comment as they jumped into the van and hoisted her bookshelf between them. Gina grabbed a heavy box of books and walked behind them as they maneuvered the shelf down the ramp and up the narrow stairs. She had been ready to chop the beloved piece of furniture into kindling after sweating through the process of loading it this morning, and in her relief at having help moving it, she let go of some of her trepidation about being with these small-town strangers.

The staircase felt more solid to her tonight, but the real surprise came when she entered the apartment for the first time. She had wanted to arrive early enough to do a thorough cleaning before moving any of her things in, but after the effort of loading the van and driving through traffic, she had decided she didn't care about grime and bits of hay. Or even spiders, for that matter. She had just wanted to get at least a few things moved in, and to worry about cleaning later.

But the apartment was spotless. The green carpet was no less threadbare and skimpy, and the linoleum no less cracked, but there wasn't a cobweb or mote of dust in sight. Even the light fixtures had been wiped clean. The cleanliness was almost too much for her to bear, when it was added to the emotional turmoil of being ousted from her life and thrust unwillingly into this rustic setting. She still hated small-town living and still wished fervently to be able to return to her bright city apartment—and she knew Wren would have been thrilled for her to go back as well—but she appreciated the expansive gestures of a clean home and helping hands to move her into it.

The swirl of emotions, from grief to gratitude, made her want to collapse in the middle of the floor and cry, but she continued to make trips to the van. Her four helpmates were like machines, carting load after load up the stairs, and they probably would have swept around her like a stream around a boulder if she gave in to her exhausted and weepy state. The least she could do was remain upright and do her part.

The twins—Mike and Liam, she learned when they were introduced in an offhand way while passing each other on the way to and from the van—were mainly interested in discussing a new four-wheeler they had acquired. Once they heard her answer to their dad's question about what she did for a living, though, they sent a barrage of questions her way about how to build their Instagram followings. She found it surprisingly easy to talk to them, and the casual monotony of carting boxes around seemed to take the pressure off.

"How'd the two of you become friends, anyway?" Mike asked, after she finished explaining the ways she liked to combine distance and close-up shots in her photo stories. He nodded his head toward Wren. "You're so different."

Were they friends? Wren gave her a sheepish sort of shrug, and Gina assumed she had told them that as a vague way of explaining her arrival here. The story might not be convincing since they really were vastly different types of people, but Gina recognized how the protective cover of friendship freed her from having to share anything more personal about her situation unless she chose to.

"You know they didn't meet on Facebook," Liam said with a laugh. "Wren probably doesn't even know what that is."

"Hey," said Wren, setting down the final box of books with a thud. "I'm a modern woman, so I know what Facebook is."

Gina shook her head in Liam's direction. "Doubtful. She probably thinks you're talking about regular books. She might possibly be familiar with those."

"Of course I am," Wren said, with a haughty expression. She turned to Gina and lowered her voice slightly. "Although I think that Gutenberg fellow is going to mess them up."

"Good one, Wren," Gina said, mimicking Wren's conspiratorial whisper. "Fifteenth-century references really help prove your point."

Nick set a lamp on the table next to Gina's small sofa. "You three shouldn't tease Wren. She really is quite progressive, you know. Just last year she got a real phone for the barn and replaced those tin cans and string she'd been using."

Wren sighed dramatically. "I miss those tin cans," she said. "No one ever called me on them and tried to sell me diet pills."

"Fair point," Gina said. She pulled her cell out of her back pocket and looked at it forlornly. "All my phone does is give me directions, let me play games, store thousands of books and photos and—"

Wren batted playfully at her hand. "My cans can multitask, too. They hold pencils, squash bugs, act as paperweights…"

Nick held up his hands in surrender. "This could go on for days, if you're going to try to convince Wren of the merit of anything that was developed after the nineteenth century. We'll leave you two to it."

Gina offered to pay them for their help, grateful beyond words that she hadn't had to leave most of her stuff in the van. She'd get through this first night much easier with her familiar furniture and books around her. Nick and the boys refused to take any money, assuring her that Wren's pizza more than covered it.

"People will do anything for pizza," Wren said once they were alone. "Let me give you a quick rundown of the place, and then I'll leave you to get some sleep."

Gina had been worried about being alone with Wren once everyone left. The others had been a good buffer, and she had been too occupied by the physical labor of moving and the conversation to do much more than notice the way Wren's muscles flexed against the fabric of her shirt and her jeans whenever she bent over to pick up a box or climbed up the van's ramp. And she barely registered the warm friction of skin on skin when their hands met as they carried Gina's dresser up the stairs. Yeah, at least two percent of the time she hardly remembered that Wren was even there.

Right now, though, she was too tired to do more than briefly imagine what it would feel like to run her hands over Wren's biceps or thighs, or how good it might be to have Wren's hands touching *her*. Those imagined sensations were going to be troublesome once Gina was rested and settled, but for now, her weariness and sadness at having traded the apartment of her dreams for this one were enough to dampen any arousal Wren might cause in her.

Plus, Wren's instructions for living in this place were a bit concerning. She seemed to have taken rural living to an extreme, and Gina's mind reeled with the explanations for dealing with solar power and well water.

"Is this supposed to be the epitome of the simple life?" she asked. "Because it seems a lot more complicated than what I'm used to."

Wren raised her arms in an expansive gesture. "There are some challenges, but living as much off the grid as I can gives me a lot more freedom."

Gina frowned, skeptical about what sort of freedom she was going to find here. As far as she was concerned, the grid was good. She really liked the grid.

"Well, I suppose I can survive here for a little while, until we get your marketing plan set up and I can move back to the city." Gina nodded, trying to draw strength from her confident sounding words. This was temporary. Like going camping or out on a survivalist retreat. It would build character. "What's the Wi-Fi password?"

Wren gave her that look again, as if she couldn't quite process the words Gina was saying. "I don't have internet."

Gina closed her eyes. Really, how much character did she want to build, anyway? "You hired me to help you build a presence on the internet. How do you expect me to do that... *without internet?*"

Wren shrugged. "I don't know. I assumed you'd do the computer stuff somewhere else."

Gina had her phone. She could survive the night, at least. She mentally repeated that several times, like a mantra, before she spoke again. "Fine. I'll pick up a mobile hotspot when I take the van back to Seattle tomorrow."

"Sounds like a plan," Wren said. "I'll pay for it while you're here—just don't expect me to use it. Oh, I'll be right back."

Gina frowned as Wren ran down the stairs. She actually did expect her to use the internet, but she wasn't going to argue about it tonight. How else did Wren think she was going to market her farm online? Apparently the tin cans weren't doing the job, otherwise Wren wouldn't have needed to hire her.

She was back in less than a minute with Grover in tow and Biscuit wriggling madly in her arms. "I had them in the tack room while we were moving so they wouldn't be in the way. I left some food and a water bowl in the cupboard under the sink that you can put out for him." She hesitated, then backed toward the door. "Well, good night, then."

"Good night. Thank you for helping unload the van."

Wren waved off her thanks and disappeared into the darkness. Gina stood on the landing for a few minutes, with Grover leaning his furry weight against her leg. The air was still and cool against her skin, and the stars seemed to drip heavily in the sky. Gina shuddered. The solid emptiness of the space around her made her feel as if she were in a sensory deprivation tank. She went inside and looked around. Boxes covered the floor and every piece of furniture except her bed. She hadn't thought to bring food with her, except for some protein bars, and who knew where they were in all this mess. She didn't feel like getting back in the van and driving miles until she found a drive-through. She would have to go to the store the next day. She went into the kitchen area and opened the fridge, as if something might magically appear, and found a grease-blotched delivery box with a large cheese pizza inside. *Wren.* Gina smiled. Apparently she hadn't been too late for dinner after all.

She took the box with her since she didn't have any plates unpacked and curled up on her bed to call Maia, who thankfully was a devout night owl. Grover jumped up and lay down close beside her, resting his chin on her hip and waiting for handouts. He was going to get white hair all over her comforter. And possibly drool. Maybe even fleas? The dogs she had known had always slept outside in kennels, never in the house. Maybe she should at least tell him to get down and sleep on the floor. She sighed instead and leaned against Grover's side, holding her phone so the dog would be the first thing Maia would see when she answered Gina's call.

CHAPTER SEVEN

Wren stumbled through her predawn rituals of feeding and turning out the horses. She had barely slept the night before, and she wasn't quite sure how Gina had managed to disturb her evening when she wasn't even visible. Wren's house was on the other side of the barn from the apartment, and she hadn't seen any sign that Gina had so much as stepped outside her door all night, but still Wren had felt her presence as sharply as if she'd been standing in the room with her, jolting her awake every time she drifted off to sleep.

She had made the mistake of spending too much time in Gina's company last night, but she wouldn't repeat the offence. Gina was fine on her own, of course— more than fine, in Wren's opinion—but sooner or later she was going to bring up the online marketing plan Dianna had concocted, and she'd expect Wren to get involved. Wren was doing her best to keep herself out of that particular equation. She had arranged for Nick and the twins to help Gina move in, and she had intended to leave the four of them to take care of the unloading without her. Five people going up and down the stairs had been inefficient, since they spent a lot of time waiting on the ground or on the landing for someone else to walk past.

Still, after everything Gina had been going through—with unknown people threatening and harassing her—Wren hadn't felt comfortable leaving her alone with three strangers, no matter how friendly and nonthreatening they were. Not that Wren was much more than a stranger to Gina, but at least she was a familiar face.

She really needn't have worried because, after an initial awkward few minutes, Gina had seemed at ease with everyone. Once she started chatting to Mike and Liam about computer stuff, her whole demeanor changed. Wren had tuned out most of the words, but she had paid closer attention to Gina's expressions and gestures than she would have liked. Her passion for what she did for a living was evident in every aspect of her voice and body language, just as it had been during her interview with Wren.

Wren didn't understand how anyone could care so much about the internet, but she really hated the person who had tried to ruin Gina's online life.

Wren shook her head as she parked the empty feed carts in the hay barn. This infatuation could be dangerous. She felt sorry for Gina, that was all. And attracted to her, naturally. Neither of those reactions to having her around could be allowed to grow, or who knew what would happen to Wren's life. Maybe she'd end up wired to the gills, with a television and computer in every room, spending her days watching other people's lives instead of living her own. Staring at the screen of a cell phone instead of looking up and into the eyes of the people around her. Not that Gina seemed to be as mind-numbed as Wren thought someone who made their living with computers would be, since she actually was quite charming around other human beings, although she might have been putting on an act around strangers. Give her time, Wren decided, and she'd reveal herself to be the screen-addicted zombie Wren expected.

Until she became an unappealing, shallow zombie, Wren

needed to avoid contact with her. They'd have to discuss the work she was going to do for the barn, of course, but maybe those marketing meetings would douse Wren's attraction. She'd be so bored by the internet-based conversation that her mind wouldn't be able to shake off its numbness and notice every detail about Gina's smile—like the way the corners of her mouth were naturally upturned as if she was always about to smile or laugh. Or the way her blue eyes reflected her amusement when they joked together about the apartment or Wren's pretend desire to have her banished from the farm.

What was more likely was that Wren's brain would ignore the computer talk and spend every ounce of its energy focused on Gina. Again, avoidance seemed to be the answer. It shouldn't be too hard since Gina was probably hidden away in the apartment right now, staring at some screen or another. Or she was going through the d.t.'s because those screens weren't connected to the internet yet. Wren had even more motivation to get her a mobile whatever-the-hell she needed, so she'd stay inside and online.

She picked up Biscuit, who had been gloomy all night with Grover gone, and carried him to the barn and the stalls she needed to clean. Wren hadn't seen one hair from Grover's furry white hide since last night, either, even though she had assumed he would be frantically searching for her this morning. The traitor.

Wren stomped into the barn, angry with herself for spending her entire morning thinking about how she needed to stop thinking about Gina. She stopped and blinked, trying to figure out what she was seeing. Gina was at the far end of the barn, just beyond the shadows where the concrete aisleway ended. She had a tripod and a chair and seemed to be talking to herself. Grover was lying on the ground at Gina's feet, and Biscuit squirmed to get free from Wren's arms. She set him down, and he raced down the aisle. Wren followed more slowly, feeling her irritation growing as she walked. She wasn't annoyed with Gina necessarily—after all, it would be ridiculous to make the area outside of her apartment off-limits to her. No, Wren's irritation was mainly self-focused. She couldn't keep her mind off Gina when she wasn't even around. How was she going to concentrate on her day, let alone find the sense of peace she always had when she had the barn to herself before clients arrived, with Gina lounging right in the middle of the barn's wide doorway?

As she got closer, her eyes adjusted to the morning light, and Gina morphed from a silhouette to a distinct person with lines and colors. She was wearing black sweatpants that sat low on her hips, and her feet were bare. Who went barefoot in a barn? Her pale yellow sweater was wide enough at the neck to drape over one shoulder and loosely knit enough to show the black sports bra she wore underneath. Her hair was piled in a bun, with all the hues of it twisting together. She was incomprehensibly putting some sort of cream on her face and talking to a small black and silver camera. She had one of Wren's extra water buckets upended next to her.

Biscuit clambered over Grover and tried to scramble onto Gina's lap. She picked up a towel off the bucket-slash-dressing table and wiped her hands before reaching down to pick him up. She rubbed his ears and kept up a constant stream of comments, lifting the small beagle until he was close enough to poke the camera lens with his nose. Great. That would probably look adorable. Biscuit, Internet Star.

"I know you're here," she said as soon as she was close enough to speak without shouting.

"Very clever of you," Gina said. She looked around her makeshift film set. "Although I am pretty hard to miss out here. Still, well done."

"That's not what I..." Wren sighed and started again. "When I told you I liked my privacy, you said I wouldn't even know you were here. Well, I know you're here."

Gina shrugged and set Biscuit down next to Grover. "I was planning to spend the day hiding in those bushes over there, but the light out here is amazing. I couldn't resist filming here."

"Yes, it's the newest technology in lighting. We call it the sun. Patent pending."

Gina turned back to face the camera. "My new landlord, everyone. Don't mind her—she's a bit cranky in the morning. And at night." She paused and glanced at Wren out of the corner of her eyes. "And in the afternoon."

Wren stepped back, unsure how wide the camera's shot was. "You are not roping me into this online business of yours."

Gina laughed. "Don't worry, I'm only teasing." She looked at the camera and made a slashing motion at her throat. "Cut that last part out. There, see? Editing Me will make sure you're not in the video, but the puppy part is staying. Seriously, though, I'm being extra careful not to have anything that could identify where I'm staying or with whom. I would never put you or your farm at risk like that."

Wren shook her head and stared over Gina's shoulder at the setting she had chosen for her sunlit backdrop. A wall of stunted fir trees grew in the harsh, rocky soil at the edge of the bay, with a lone madrone arched like a frame over the glimpse of water. It was beautiful. Generic, for Washington State, but beautiful. Gina had had her life turned upside down by this unknown person, but here she was worrying about protecting Wren's identity.

"To be honest, I'd love a chance to meet the coward who wrote those things about you face-to-face." She looked back at Gina in time to see her eyes widen slightly at Wren's words, as if surprised by the vehemence in her voice. Wren cleared her throat and reverted to cranky. "What kind of videos do you make, anyway? I thought you did things about living in the city and painting furniture. I didn't realize Morning Ablutions at the Barn was in your repertoire."

Gina sighed and leaned forward to push a button on her camera. "I have a feeling this might take some time to explain," she said as she sat down again. She waved in the direction of the camera. "I don't want my battery to run down while you're making fun of me. Batteries are newfangled contraptions that make things go."

The last sentence was delivered in the tone of someone speaking to a three-year-old. Wren laughed. "Well, I hadn't been planning on making fun of you, but I definitely will now. Go ahead, amuse me with your weird internet activities."

"It's a Get Ready With Me video. I saw them a lot on YouTube when I was researching popular clips and planning my own content. Usually they involve putting on a bunch of makeup, which isn't my style, so I didn't think I'd ever make one, but I got requests from my followers for this type of chatty video. I gave one a try and had fun with it. Mostly I just talk about what's going on in my life, but sometimes I have people post questions and I answer them." She held up her hand as if in warning. "I know what you're going to say, so don't bother."

Wren frowned. She had no idea what she was going to say. The thought of filming herself having a conversation with a camera while she got ready to go out and do barn chores was the most ludicrous thing she could imagine. At least it would be a short video since she barely did more than brush her teeth before feeding her horses. They really didn't care about mascara or combed hair, and neither did she. "I'm speechless," Wren finally managed to say. "What part of this is fun for you?"

Gina bent down to pet Grover, and he immediately rolled onto his back for a belly rub. "Mainly, it's a great source of revenue for me. I review products and get paid through affiliate links and sponsorships. Personally, it's sort of therapeutic, I guess. I can relax and talk, without worrying about what I say since none of it is live. A lot gets edited out, and sometimes I don't even post the footage, which is what happened with the last two I did, while I was dealing with the doxing and the move and everything. I just deleted them. This one feels more...normal, I suppose. Or more in control. So I should be able to post it."

Biscuit was starting to sniff the tripod, which probably would lead to trying to dismantle it with his teeth, so Wren sat on the gravel next to Grover and pulled the puppy onto her lap. She really should be cleaning stalls right now, but this was much more fascinating. It was like watching a nature documentary on strange internet dwellers. She'd count it as research into a bizarre human lifestyle, and her interest had absolutely nothing to do with wanting to know more about Gina.

"Are you sure it's safe to share too much about yourself with a bunch of strangers? You don't even know these people, so how can you trust them?"

Gina shrugged. "They're my friends. Some are colleagues, and others are more like clients, I suppose. Most of them are really nice and positive—one wasn't. I won't give up my life—my career—or all the good people who are interested in my content, just because of one bad person. But like I said, I'm more aware now of what my followers will see and hear. I'll be cautious, but I won't give up everything in my life because of this. And I won't accept that it's my fault and change who I am or what I post or how I present myself."

"Of course it's not your fault," Wren said. She admired the bravery Gina was showing in this situation, even though she still didn't get the allure of the online life that seemed to make Gina thrive. She didn't have to understand it to want to defend Gina's right to make her own choices. She reached over and placed her hand on top of Gina's where it rested on Grover's side, tilting forward to get Gina to look at her. "When I asked if it was safe, I didn't mean to imply that you were doing anything that encouraged this kind of hate. I just don't want you to be hurt."

Maybe she had been wrong to want Gina to look at her. Those expressive eyes reflected her emotions too clearly, whether she was showing defiance or humor or, like now, another jolt of surprise at Wren's words. Wren pulled her hand away and turned her attention back to Biscuit. "I mean, I wouldn't want anyone to be hurt. Really, if you decide you want to stare cross-eyed at the camera for an hour and call it performance art, I'll support your right to be strange." Wren laughed, determined to return to banter and leave this awkward seriousness behind. "Not that what you're doing isn't strange enough as it is. Putting on face cream and fixing your hair, like you're having a slumber party with the entire internet."

Wren gave an exaggerated eye roll in case her words didn't convey how ridiculous this was to her. Gina sat up and laughed with her, shoving her shoulder playfully. "I'd never put it that way, but you're right. It's getting together with friends in a way I can't when it's in person."

"But it's fake. They're not real friends, and you're sharing an edited version of yourself." Wren winced after she said the words. She really wanted to try to understand what Gina was finding in the online world of hers, but she had spoken without thinking first. Gina didn't seem to find Wren's comments offensive, though. She tipped her head to one side in a thoughtful way.

"No," she finally said. "I'm *more* me. I might edit out some *ums* or some overly personal comments I let slip, but not much else. When I'm with other people, my shyness can get in the way. I'm not the person I want to be, the person I am inside my head. But when I talk to the camera, even though I'm aware that thousands of people will watch me, I can access my real self and be funny or serious without the barriers of hesitation and doubt in the way."

Wren was intrigued by the image of a screen breaking down barriers with other people. She didn't understand it, since the opposite would be true for her. "You don't seem to have any trouble dredging up insults to fling in my direction," she said. She tried to make herself sound wounded by the easy way Gina was able to tease her, but instead she felt curiously warmed by the thought that, for whatever reason, Gina didn't need a lens between them in order to be herself. That thread of thought was a dangerous one, and Wren intentionally stopped tugging at it. "And last night, you didn't seem uncomfortable with Nick and the boys."

"You're different," Gina said. She had leaned back in her chair, but now she sat up straight, and Wren sensed a new stiffness in her. "All of you, I mean. All four of you. You were helping me, and the situation was unusual. Plus, it was late, and I was too exhausted to be awkward."

Wren nodded as if it all made sense to her. Gina waved at her camera. "I should finish this," she said. "It'll look strange if the video starts in the morning, and then it's suddenly midafternoon after only a few minutes. Besides, I need to get the van back into the city."

Wren nodded and stood up. "I need to get to work, too. I've

been trying to train Grover and Biscuit to clean the stalls for me, but they refuse to help." She turned to walk away, waiting for a sense of relief since she was escaping a conversation that had skimmed on the verge of an intimacy she had no interest in pursuing. She had done her part, hadn't she? She had given Gina a job and had arranged for moving help. If she made any more efforts to be around her, they wouldn't be able to be explained away as common courtesy but would mean she just wanted to spend time with her. And that was bad, no matter how tasty Gina smelled with her honey-scented creams and potions, or how the way she shared her vulnerability with Wren only seemed to prove how strong she was.

She was about to launch into her mental lecture about how different they were, blah, blah, blah, but she spun on her heel and faced Gina again. She hadn't started filming yet and was quietly watching Wren stand in the barn aisle like a fool.

"Let me know when you're ready to go," she said. "I'll follow and drive you to wherever you've parked your car."

"Oh, you really don't have to go with me," Gina said, holding up both hands as if they were shields. "I can get a ride from the rental place."

"That's me. I'm your ride. Plus, we need to buy you that mobile internet thing so you can get to work on marketing me." She paused and squinted at Gina. She seemed to be handling the lack of internet with surprising calmness. "You haven't been online for hours now. I'd expect you to be tragically weeping, or maybe writhing on the floor in agony."

Gina made a scoffing noise. "Please. I like being online, but I can live without it." She paused and gave Wren a sheepish look, picking up the cell phone that was on her lap and wiggling it in Wren's direction. "Besides, I can access the internet with my phone. I've been doing Google searches the whole time we've been talking."

Wren laughed and shook her head. "It's an addiction," she said as she walked away.

"It's my career," Gina called after her.

"Sorry about the interruption." Wren heard Gina loudly addressing her camera again. "That was my newest client. I'm supposed to somehow make her an appealing online presence. Trust me, friends, that's going to take a miracle."

"Edit that out," Wren called over her shoulder.

Chapter Eight

G ina managed to finish filming her video, but once she was done she had little recollection of what she had said after Wren walked away, and she escaped back to the apartment as soon as she could. She'd see what she could salvage while editing, but she had a feeling this was another one that would never be uploaded.

She had known from the moment she got out of her car that she was attracted to Wren. She had even been aware of how easy it had been to talk to her during the interview, which was surprising on its own, and even more so when Gina factored in how often her thoughts strayed in uncomfortable, nonprofessional directions while they were talking. Until Wren had pointed it out today, though, she hadn't quite grasped the extent to which she felt at ease around Wren.

She could talk to almost anyone—in person or online, stranger or friend—as long as the topic was restricted to social media or some other aspect of her internet life, like the Instagram advice she had given Mike and Liam last night. But today she had shared with Wren the reasons behind her role as an online personality and the parts of her real-life character that she thought were lacking or just plain inferior. She didn't even talk about those aspects of herself to Maia, whom she considered to be a close friend. And as much as they connected with each other, Gina had serious concerns about how awkward the encounter might be if she and Maia were to meet in person. She knew herself too well to believe she could overcome her naturally awkward nature no matter how much she liked another person.

With Wren, it was as if none of it mattered. If Gina thought of a retort to one of Wren's antisocial comments, she simply said it. When Wren had sat next to her today and made her the sole focus of her laser-like attention, Gina had answered her questions and talked about herself without activating the filters she usually had in place.

Gina tucked the last stack of books onto her shelf and broke down the cardboard box. She had been puttering around in the apartment ever since she had dismantled her impromptu set this morning, unpacking and storing the items she would need for the next few weeks or so. Most of the boxes remained full, piled against the wall in the kitchen area. She wanted to be ready to leave as soon as she decided where she was going to go, and what her next step in life should be.

She went to the window and peered out. One corner of the riding arena was visible from here, and every once in a while, she saw Wren trot by on one of the horses. Even from a distance, there was a vibrancy about her that was magnetic to Gina. She had joked about how hard it would be to make Wren look appealing online, but it wouldn't take any effort at all. Wren would be stunning in photos and videos. Gina's real challenge would be controlling her jealousy when women from all over the Northwest started flinging themselves at her, signing up for lessons just for a chance to be near her. Gina could imagine taking one of those lessons, too, and she pictured Wren standing close to her as she explained some of the finer points of riding. Putting her hands on Gina's thigh and calf to demonstrate the correct leg position...

Gina stepped back quickly when Wren cantered into view on a brown horse, as if she might look up and see Gina's thoughts through the window. She nearly tripped over Grover, who was taking the task of protecting her very seriously. He hadn't let her out of his sight since the evening before.

She stood in the center of the apartment, searching for a reason to delay, but nothing came to mind. Besides, she was hungry since she had finished the last of the cold pizza for breakfast, and her protein bars were still MIA. Maybe Wren had changed her mind about going into Seattle with her, and Gina could make the trip in familiar solitude.

Grover followed her cheerfully down the stairs, and they came around the corner of the barn just as Wren was riding her horse up from the arena. He shied at their sudden appearance, moving sideways as quickly as a cat, but Wren barely moved in the saddle as she got him back under control. Once he was standing still and looked calm, she dismounted and pulled the reins over his head.

"Were you waiting there just to leap out at us?" Wren asked as she led the horse into the barn.

"We're in the middle of nowhere. I've got to find some way to amuse myself," Gina said, following Wren down the aisle and making a determined effort to look anywhere but at Wren's ass and those sexy muscles she must have gotten from long hours in the saddle. Gina closed her eyes briefly to reorient herself. "Maybe if I add a shriek next time, I can scare the horse enough so you fall off. Oof!"

Gina opened her eyes again, a little too late. Wren was watching her with an amused expression on her face.

"Was that a demonstration of the shriek, or did you just run into the back of my horse?"

"I didn't realize you had stopped," Gina said, laughing as she moved a safer distance from the animal. Well, she had been worried about feeling too comfortable around Wren. Awkwardness restored.

Wren shook her head, as if Gina's blundering around the barn was just another of her unfathomable quirks. She put her horse in the crossties and started to remove the saddle. "I'll just finish putting him away, and then we can go."

"Don't you have lessons to teach, or something?" Gina asked, gingerly taking the sweaty saddle pad and heavy saddle when Wren handed them to her.

Wren shook her head, gesturing at a metal saddle rack near the office. "It's Monday," she said, as if that explained everything.

Gina set the saddle in place and flipped the pad upside down before draping it over the saddle, so the sweat could start to dry and wouldn't damage the leather. "What's Monday got to do with anything?"

"You ride horses," Wren said instead of answering Gina's question, watching her arrange the saddle and pad.

"I grew up in a small town outside of Moses Lake." Which, in turn, was a small town outside of Spokane, in eastern Washington. If towns were Russian nesting dolls, Gina came from the innermost one. Tiny and solid, with nothing interesting inside. "I took barrel racing for a PE credit in junior high, so yes, I've ridden before, but I don't anymore. It's not something I particularly enjoyed."

Wren remained silent, but she raised her eyebrows in a questioning way, as if she sensed that Gina had more to say on the subject.

She sighed and continued. "The things we were taught, and the way the other kids rode…it just seemed very rough, and even cruel at times. I wasn't happy with any of it. It just… the whole experience left a bad taste behind."

Wren nodded, as if sensing the rest of the story in between the words. "Did you tell the other kids how you felt?"

Gina nodded. And then horses had gone on the don't-touch-the-subject list along with hunting dogs. "Nothing changed, except they had another reason to tease me. As if being a shy, bookish lesbian wasn't enough." She paused. Was there any way to keep herself from sharing everything with Wren? She thought she saw anger flash in Wren's expression, but she wasn't sure. "I hope I'm not offending you. It seems like you do things differently here, but maybe I shouldn't have said anything—"

Wren held up a hand and took a step closer to her. "Some people see riding as a partnership, but others see it as a power trip. A chance to dominate another creature. Promise you'll tell me if you ever think I'm being rough or cruel with my animals?"

Gina nodded, not quite trusting herself to speak. As little as she knew about Wren, she couldn't imagine ever needing to speak up in that way. Still, she was glad she had spoken up when she was younger, no matter the reception her words had gotten. The experience had been one of her catalyst moments, making her more determined than ever to escape her narrow-minded world and find the place where she truly belonged. She didn't care whether that new place was virtual or not—it was hers.

"So…Mondays?"

Wren nodded and moved away, toward her horse again, looking as relieved as Gina felt for the subject to change away from the heavy topic. "Weekends tend to be really busy for competition and training barns. Most shows are held over the weekend, and schoolkids and working adults have more time for lessons than they do on weekdays, so my farm is closed on

Mondays to give me a chance to catch up on training rides and school my own horses." She paused and sighed dramatically. "And to give me some much needed alone time."

"Must be your favorite day of the week," Gina guessed.

Wren leaned around her horse to give Gina a pointed stare. "Used to be," she said.

Gina laughed. She'd much rather have Wren reiterating how much she wanted her privacy than working whatever magic she possessed to make Gina talk about herself. And her small-town childhood, for God's sake, which was a subject she usually avoided. She tried to keep the focus off herself while she watched Wren finish grooming her horse. "Would you really be happier if you lived out here alone?"

Wren flashed a somewhat sheepish grin in her direction. "No, of course not. Not completely, at least. I like my clients, but I also like having time when the farm is quiet and the horses and I can recharge after lessons or shows. If all your marketing turned this into a McFarm with billions served, we'd lose some of that balance, and everyone would suffer for it."

"By *billions*, do you mean the ten new students Dianna wants you to get?"

Wren nodded with a long-suffering sigh. "Yes. Some days I think even one extra might push me over the edge." She paused and stared into the distance as if rethinking her response. "Unless they have a really amazing horse, though. Then I wouldn't mind just one new client."

Gina frowned. She was filing away the information Wren was doling out in between sarcastic remarks, and later she would use it to build a marketing plan tailored just for her. Wren's statement didn't seem to fit with the picture Gina was forming of her. "An amazing horse?" she repeated. "So you're looking for a higher class of client, someone more competitive?"

Wren tossed her brush into the grooming box. "Not necessarily. Amazing, as in lots of fun to ride. Or a quirky one that's a challenge to train. Some of my riders want to compete at high levels, while others just show for fun. Some, like Dianna, don't have any interest in competing but just want to learn and grow. I don't care what their goals are, but I do care about having enough time and energy to devote to each one."

Gina smiled to herself as Wren put her horse in its stall. She had been thrown by the idea that Wren might want some fancy new clients, but her clarification of the point made more sense to Gina. She just had to prove to Wren that she had a better chance of finding students with similar interests and a like-minded desire to improve if she showcased her farm and her skills in detail online, rather than confining herself to the people who randomly chose her farm out of the yellow pages. Not that Wren was likely to answer the phone when they called, she decided as it started ringing when they walked past the office.

"We're going the long way around?" Wren asked, ignoring the call and heading out to the van.

"Yes, unless you know of someone who can paddle us across the Sound on a big raft. I assumed you wouldn't want to go on the ferry, what with those big modern engines strapped to the back."

"Funny. I assumed we were going the long way because you might drive that big van right through the railing and into the water, what with the tiny city car you usually drive."

Gina elbowed her in the side, not wanting to admit she had been worried about doing exactly that last night. She had occasionally forgotten she was driving something three times the length of her own car, so she hadn't wanted to add a narrow, bouncy ferry ramp to the equation.

"I do just fine in the van, thank you. Let's see if you can

keep up with me." Gina scrunched her nose as she replayed those words in her mind. She hadn't meant for them to sound as suggestive as they did. Wren paused long enough to let Gina know she heard the double meaning as well, and then she nodded at the van and her older blue Ford pickup.

"I don't think either of us is going to set a speed record today, but maybe I'll take you up on that challenge once we get to know each other a little better."

Gina opened her mouth to offer a retort but then closed it again because nothing came to mind except *I hope you do.* Even if they had been separated by the comforting vastness of the internet, she wouldn't have been able to come up with a less eager sounding comeback.

She spent most of the drive wondering her way through various scenarios in which she and Wren had a chance to take their sparring relationship into the bedroom. None of them were sound and sensible options, but they were fun to explore. The last ten minutes before they reached the rental place were filled with stern lectures to herself about why sex with Wren was a bad idea. None of her mind's arguments convinced her body, but the mental exercise cooled her off enough to get through the next part of their excursion.

After she had turned in the van's keys—with no small measure of relief—Gina climbed into Wren's truck and gave her directions for getting to the nearest Best Buy. She looked around the interior of the pickup as they drove, and it was exactly what she would have expected Wren to drive. Bare-bones, but fairly tidy except for the inevitable hay stems and mud stains on the floor mats.

"You don't even have a radio," she said, pointing at the bare expanse of dashboard. She hadn't thought Wren would add on any extras, but she thought most cars came standard with at least a radio. "Do you sing a cappella while you're driving, or do you exist in a world where music hasn't been invented yet?"

Wren grinned. "I spend my time thinking profound thoughts. A skill which has been lost to the computer generations."

Gina gave a snort of laughter. "Profound thoughts, my ass. You're probably thinking about all the butter you have to churn when you get home, and whether you'll have enough daylight left over to get down to the river and beat your laundry on a rock."

"Well, your ass is wrong," Wren said, slapping her gently on the thigh, high enough for Gina to know where her thoughts were heading. "I don't use a rock. I gave in last year and bought one of those high-tech washboards."

Wren parked in the Best Buy lot, as far from the door as she could get, probably in case the technology tried to seep out the door and attack her.

"I'll wait here," she said. She reached into her pocket and pulled out a handful of cash. "Here you go."

Gina looked at the bills in her hand and shook her head. "You're coming, too. We should look at a laptop for you."

Wren gave her a look of pure horror, and Gina had to laugh. "Something simple, I promise. You'll need to keep up with the social media accounts I create for you. Post new content, reply to comments. Easy stuff."

"That's your job, isn't it?"

"For now, yes. But once I come back to Seattle, I won't have new things to post unless you email me photos and blogs. You need a computer to do that, and then you might as well use it to do the posting yourself. I'll explain everything to you, so it will be simple."

Wren gave her an exasperated look. "Simplicity isn't the issue. I know I'm capable of doing it. I just don't want to."

Gina shrugged and started counting the money Wren had given her. "You sound scared to me."

"Am I twelve? Do you really think calling me a chicken will make me want to do this?"

Gina looked at her without answering, and eventually Wren made a growling kind of noise and opened her door. "I'll come with you, but only because I can't continue to have this conversation. Not because you said I'm scared." She got out of the truck and looked back at Gina. "And I'm not buying a computer."

Gina got out of the truck and jogged to catch up to her. "It's okay. We'll just walk past the laptops really slowly today. Next time we can walk through the section. Maybe even touch one of them, if you're feeling brave."

"It's a matter of principle, not fear," Wren said as they stepped through the door into the brightly lit version of Wren hell, complete with one hundred television sets all showing a different montage of visual effects.

She seemed disoriented, so Gina grabbed her sleeve and tugged her toward the far side of the store. "Let me guess— you were raised on a commune by hippie parents who told you technology was evil," she said as they passed the cameras. She would have liked to stop and browse, but she'd wait until she was here without Wren to comparison shop for new equipment.

"Not even close," Wren said. "My parents own SoarInc."

This time it was Gina who felt disoriented as she came to a stop next to a rack of phone cases. "Your parents are *those* Lindleys? Are you kidding?"

"You've heard of them, I take it," Wren said with a wry smile.

Obviously there were some underlying issues between Wren and her parents, which had resulted in their daughter turning her back on the entire tech world. Gina tried to curb her excitement about being close to someone who had sprung from the brilliant Lindley family, but she wasn't very successful. She at least managed to stop hopping from foot to foot.

"They revolutionized wrapper technology. I used their methods when I first learned how to code, and I designed the most amazing website using...oh." Using WREN. She put her hand over her mouth, unsure whether she was horrified or about to burst into laughter.

"Using their Wrapper Encoding System," Wren finished for her. "Yes, I've heard of it."

Gina pulled Wren to one side, out of the way of a man who was trying to get past them. "I thought you were named after a bird."

"Most people do. I usually don't bother to correct them. Can we get this done and get out of here?"

"Yes, of course," Gina said. She had a lot of questions— including *Will your parents be stopping by anytime soon so I can meet them?*—but they could wait until later. "Right over here."

"I'm surprised you've heard about WREN, since it was created before you were born. It's older than I am, and I'm prehistoric in computer years. Do you still use it?"

"Not WREN, of course, but I've always kept up with the latest versions," Gina said absently as she hurriedly looked through the selection of mobile routers. "Right now I'm using...never mind. Ouch."

"What do you mean, ouch?" Wren asked.

"We want this one." Gina handed her a hard plastic package and started walking toward the front of the store. "It's just...well, the newest version is called Falcon."

Wren stopped again. "Falcons *eat* wrens."

"I'm sorry," Gina said, bumping Wren with her shoulder and getting her walking again. She glanced sideways at her. "You must have the most uncomfortable family dinners."

Wren had been looking slightly traumatized, but at Gina's comment she let out a burst of laughter. "You have no idea," she said. "And trust me, this Thanksgiving is going to be a doozy."

Gina laughed along with her, relieved to see her relax. She and Wren paid at the register, and Gina didn't even mention her intended walk past the computer section. She figured Wren had had enough computer talk for one day.

CHAPTER NINE

Gina slid into the truck's passenger seat and settled back with the router in a bag on her lap, prepared for a silent drive to the hotel. Wren was most likely still imagining the bird carnage caused by her parents' falcon, and Gina herself wasn't in the best of moods. She was leaving the city behind for good now—temporarily, but thoroughly. Her belongings were settled in Wren's barn, and soon she and her car would be farm residents. She had felt a sense of straddling worlds last night, with her vehicle still bonding her to the city somehow, but now she would be in Poulsbo with no real reason to come back to Seattle. She would have to return to the city regularly for meetings and receptions, of course, and she could come back for personal errands anytime she wanted, but she would no longer feel like a resident once her car left the hotel parking lot. She needed time to process her impending solar-powered doom, and Wren had her own feathered demons to contemplate.

She gave Wren directions to the hotel and then lapsed into her planned silence, which lasted for the five seconds it took Wren to maneuver out of the parking lot and onto the street. Gina realized she felt tired more than sad, and her mind was spinning with to-do lists that included unpacking, reading and responding to thousands of her followers' comments, and potentially redefining her entire online content to match her new lifestyle. She needed distraction, not extra time to dwell on the tasks ahead, especially when she couldn't do much about them until she was back in the apartment with her laptop. She glanced over at Wren, who really did look upset and like she could benefit from getting her mind off their conversation.

"We might as well use this time for work," Gina said. "Why don't we brainstorm some ideas for your blog?" She smacked Wren lightly on the arm with the router package. "Stop making that face. I'm not asking you to talk about computers, but about horses. You just need to think about some riding or training topics, and I'll do the posting."

For now. She didn't say it out loud, but eventually she'd get Wren to do the basic work of maintaining her farm's online presence. One baby step at a time, though.

Wren exhaled audibly. "I really wouldn't know what to say. I mean, there are plenty of fascinating aspects of dressage, but who'd want to read me rambling on about them?"

"You'll be surprised," Gina said, looking out the front window and remembering the first real connections she had made online. The first moments when she had recognized that she could find friends who shared her interests and beliefs— or who respected her for having them, even if they weren't exactly the same as everyone else's. "I guarantee you'll find people who not only want to hear what you have to say, but who will want to engage with you in interesting conversations. That's the beauty of the internet."

"The beauty of the internet?" Wren repeated, shaking her head. "You really see it as something positive, don't you? That must be why you're hugging that thing we just bought."

Gina was about to protest, but Wren's comment had made her realize how tightly she was clutching the bag. It was her link to the online world she had created, and it was the only thing that would make life across the Sound bearable for her.

Well, besides Wren. Gina was starting to look forward to the unsettled way her insides felt when Wren was physically close to her, and to the way Wren made her laugh. Computers and her online life were too much a part of her to ever want to lose, but she could do it if she had to. She had a feeling Wren was the kind of addiction that would be impossible to shake once it took hold. Gina just had to make sure she never got close enough to lose herself to Wren.

"I'm not hugging it." Gina loosened her hold on the bag slightly and assumed as haughty a tone as she could. "I'm cradling it lovingly, just like you'd do with your favorite pair of riding boots. Now stop stalling and come up with some blog ideas."

"Ooh, sorry, but I can't. I stalled just long enough," Wren said, turning on her blinker and pulling into the hotel's parking lot.

Gina looked away from Wren and at her surroundings in surprise. She had expected a dragged-out, quiet ride, but the few miles had flown by. She frowned, unable to explain to herself why she felt so uncomfortable being comfortable with Wren. The notion sounded ridiculous in her mind, but still, she couldn't shake her disquiet.

"Hey, I'm just kidding," Wren said, apparently misinterpreting Gina's expression. "Why don't we take the ferry back to Bremerton, and I promise I'll come up with some ideas along the way. There shouldn't be too much of a line at the dock this time of day, and we'll save a lot of driving time, too."

"Um...sure," Gina said. She had no reason to insist on driving the long way through Tacoma, unless she wanted to admit her conflicted feelings to Wren. No way was that going to happen. "I'll follow you there."

The job of maneuvering through heavy city traffic as they

neared the ferry docks didn't leave Gina with much time for
worrying about her interest in Wren. Two days of inching
along in her car and the rental van were enough to make her
long for the option to be on one of the city's questionably clean
buses. Finally, she edged her car onto the ferry behind Wren's
truck and breathed a sigh of relief. She'd have more driving
to do once they reached Bremerton, but traffic would be much
lighter.

She got out of her car, ready to climb the stairs to the
ferry's top deck, and watched as Wren stepped on the truck's
back tire and swung herself into the bed of the pickup. She
reached out her hand toward Gina.

"It'll be windy up top," Wren said when Gina just stared
at her instead of taking her hand. "And we have the best view
from here. Come on."

Gina hesitated a moment longer, then took Wren's hand
and stretched to get her foot onto the truck's tall tire without
falling backward. Wren's grip was just the same as Gina
remembered from the day they met. Strong, slightly rough from
working on the farm and riding. Confident. Gina managed to
follow Wren's method of ascent, but she was trying too hard to
ignore how good Wren's skin felt against her palm to be able
to imitate her gracefulness as well. She pulled her hand free
from Wren's a moment too soon, catching her foot on the side
of the bed and falling forward.

Wren caught her with her hands around Gina's waist, her
face just inches from Gina's. Gina had thought Wren's hand felt
good holding hers, but it was nothing compared to the feeling
of those same strong hands resting just above her hip bones.
She caught herself just as she was lowering her gaze toward
Wren's mouth and moved suddenly out of Wren's grasp.

She had expected to feel some resistance as she pulled
away, but Wren had started moving at the same time, as if

feeling the same awkwardness as Gina. Gina had to laugh as they jolted away from each other like they had received electric shocks, both nearly toppling over their respective sides of the truck since there wasn't much room to back up.

She looked over her shoulder toward the stairs leading to the upper decks and saw several other passengers watching them. She looked back at Wren, still chuckling. "They probably think we're doing some weird choreographed dance up here."

Wren grinned and bowed toward their small crowd, receiving a smattering of applause and laughter. "Maybe we should sit down before we dance ourselves right off the truck."

She sat down on a pile of horse blankets and rested her back against the cab. She gestured at the place next to her, and Gina sat down, keeping at least a few inches of space between them. Her laughter faded a bit as she thought about where she was—sitting on horse blankets in the back of a pickup as she was being ferried to her new small-town home. This moment was about as far from the ideal life she had always pictured as it was possible to get.

She felt her expression settle into a smile. No, this wasn't her life's goal, but she'd get back on track. And right now, she could feel Wren's warmth next to her even though they weren't touching. And the view really was amazing. Gina's car was the last in their row, and from their position in the truck they could see over it, beyond to the Seattle skyline framed in the wide mouth of the ferry. The city was softened by dusk, and the buildings were lit with artificial lights and the glow of the setting sun. Yes, Gina was moving away from Seattle and toward a tiny farm apartment, but she didn't feel like fighting the contentment growing inside her.

Wren cleared her throat. "So, I guess I'm ready to talk about this horrid computer stuff."

"That's the spirit," Gina said. "I really like the positive

approach you're taking to this. Maybe the title of your first post could be 'I'm the best dressage instructor ever, but I really don't want you at my farm, so scram.'"

"Hmm, that has promise. We shouldn't let people know I'm the best, though. They might be willing to put up with my endearing grumpiness just for the privilege of training with me."

Gina gave a snort of laughter. "Yeah, that's a real risk. How about we say you're just mediocre?"

"Mediocre and overpriced," Wren amended. She bumped Gina with her elbow. "Now we're on the same page."

Gina jostled her in return. "Now we're on the same screen, you mean."

"I didn't mean that in the least."

Gina smiled in response, but she couldn't manage a snappy comeback since her mind was focused on the fiery sensation in her arm where it was resting against Wren's. Somewhere during their playful pushing, one of them had made contact and hadn't moved away again. Gina was pretty sure it had been her, but she wasn't prepared to admit it. And she couldn't move now, since they had been sitting this way for too many seconds to separate without it seeming awkward. She could handle a little touching, couldn't she?

"Well?" Wren asked.

Apparently Gina *couldn't* handle a little touching. She seemed to have missed part of the conversation. "Well, what? I couldn't hear you over the engines. They're very loud down here."

Wren raised her eyebrows, as if surprised by Gina's obvious lie. Gina hadn't had any problem hearing over the engines during the rest of their talk. The only trouble had come when her heart had started pounding because of Wren's nearness.

"I said, I'm very interested in the historical debate between the French and German training methods."

"You don't have to shout," Gina said. "I can hear just fine now. We must have been accelerating or something for a minute there."

Wren didn't make a comment, but she let a few seconds pass before she spoke again, in a normal tone of voice. "Anyway, I can talk about this for hours. You could ask my students, but they usually fall asleep after three minutes or so, so they probably can't attest to how long-winded I actually can be. The end of the blog can be a suggestion that the readers move to Europe to do their own research on the topic, bypassing my farm completely on their way."

Gina grinned and felt Wren's answering laughter vibrate gently through their arms, where they were in contact. The feeling frayed her already hypersensitive nerve endings. She gave in to the need for distance and shifted an inch or so away, turning toward Wren as if the sole reason she had moved was to face her.

"You can tackle major topics, but you'll need to do it in small chunks. Try starting with simple advice, like 'Five tips for finding an instructor who isn't me.'"

"I like it," Wren said, nodding thoughtfully. "How about 'Three exercises for improving the extended trot, so you can run away from my farm even faster'?"

Gina pulled out her phone and opened a note-taking app. Wren might be teasing about these titles—possibly—but once her jokes were cleared of their playfully misanthropic additions, they would probably reveal topics of real interest to her. "Keep talking," she said, tapping on her screen and trying to ignore the fact that her shift to face Wren had brought their knees in contact. They were proving to be even more distracting than arms.

"Really. You're going to help me post a blog about trotting away from my farm."

Gina made an ambivalent gesture, somewhere between a nod and a shake of her head. "I might do some minor editorial tweaking of the title. And probably most of your other sentences. Nothing you need to worry about. Now tell me more ways you can get people to improve as they're riding away from you."

❖

Wren carefully maneuvered her truck along the ramp leading to the ferry dock. She had teased Gina about driving the rental van off the boat and into the water, and now she felt in real danger of doing the same thing. Half an hour of sitting next to Gina, with various parts of their bodies touching, had gotten her so addled she was worried she might get the gas and brake pedals confused.

She figured Gina had brought up the idea of brainstorming equestrian topics more to get Wren's mind off computers and her parents than because she really felt like discussing work. And Wren had agreed to talk about those looming blog posts because she didn't want to hurt Gina's feelings or snub her when she was obviously exhausted from her move yet was still making an attempt to help Wren. Surprisingly, the conversation had been fun, and Wren really had appreciated having something else to think about besides her childhood. Even better, by the time they reached Bremerton, Gina looked more relaxed, and the tight lines of weariness around her eyes and mouth had smoothed out again.

All good things. They had talked and laughed, and both seemed to enjoy their time together. Wren should feel... well, something positive, at least. Satisfied, maybe. Elated?

Possibly. Instead, she had a vague sense of unease in the pit of her stomach. She knew Gina didn't want to be here. She didn't want a relationship with a country woman. If they misguidedly let their attraction take over, the relationship would have nowhere to go once Gina's time on the farm was over. Wren wasn't the quick fling type, although she was quick to get out of relationships when she realized they weren't destined to last forever because she didn't want to waste her own or anyone's time if emotions weren't going to go beyond surface level. She'd prefer to be alone rather than invest in another person with less than her whole heart. Nothing in her world was temporary or meaningless—her life had been devoted to the quest for depth and tradition. Talking about her parents had only served to remind her of what she valued in life, and what she believed was missing from trendy pastimes. Not that Gina seemed shallow or meaningless in any way—she was the complete opposite, in fact. But even though she was an exception, Wren had no doubt she'd choose her virtual lifestyle over Wren's simple country one without hesitation. She didn't like how ready she felt to compromise just for a chance to get closer to Gina.

Wren checked her rearview mirror to make sure Gina was close behind before she accelerated onto the highway toward Poulsbo. Gina had said she wanted to stop for a few groceries, so Wren had offered to lead her to a store. A completely unnecessary gesture, of course, since she could easily have given Gina directions. Hell, they had already passed two stores in just the few minutes they'd been off the ferry. Gina was from Seattle, not an alien planet—she most likely could identify shops which sold food just as well as Wren.

Still, Wren couldn't seem to stop herself from wanting to spend time with Gina. She parked in front of her favorite tiny store and hesitated before she got out of the truck, trying to examine her real motives in bringing Gina here. Was this a kind attempt to help Gina pick up some groceries quickly, without the need to push through the crowds in a larger store? Or was she trying to prove once and for all to Gina just how small-town she really was?

She got out of her truck and walked over to stand next to Gina, who was staring at the store as if it really was alien to her.

"Where are we?" she asked.

Wren took her elbow and urged her across the tiny parking lot. "It's a community called Scandia," she said. "I do most of my shopping in Poulsbo, but when I just want to save time and grab a few items, I come here. Buying local, you know."

"It looks smaller than a gas station convenience store."

"Wait until you're inside. It's bigger than it looks," Wren said, managing to get a reluctant Gina through the front door. Gina looked skeptical, which was only fitting since the store really was just as small as it looked from the outside. Wren waved at the teenager who was standing at the register. "Hi, Aimee."

"Hi, Ms. Lindley."

Wren laughed at Gina's sigh. She grabbed a handbasket and followed her down the baking aisle. "Is that what you don't like about small towns? Everyone knows your name and your business?"

Gina stopped and crossed her arms over her chest. "That's part of it," she said. "But mainly, I don't like having my tastes and my way of life dictated to me. You don't have choices in a community like this because you only have limited options presented to you. So instead of having raw cacao powder in my morning oatmeal, I have to either use whatever processed, sugary option is available or go without. I know my example is just one meal and doesn't really matter, but it applies to more than food. It's the principle of the thing."

Wren reached past Gina, close enough for her hand to brush against Gina's shoulder and skim lightly over her hair. She pulled a package off the shelf and handed it to Gina.

"Is this what you were looking for?"

"Crap. Yes, thank you." Gina tossed the bag of cacao powder into the basket Wren was holding.

"Sorry," said Wren. "It's hard to be indignant when you're getting what you want. If it helps, I can be upset because this store is dictating that I eat nasty powder that probably tastes nothing like chocolate when I'd rather have some processed, sugary...Oh, wait. They have that, too."

Gina bumped against her, turning her toward the back of the store. "Let's go see if they have almond milk. If I'm lucky, they won't, and I can continue my speech in the dairy aisle."

Wren smiled. Score one for the tiny town.

CHAPTER TEN

Wren trotted down the long side of the rectangular arena, keeping Foam's gait cadenced and steady. Around the corner, without letting him lean to the inside. Straight again, then forward to an extended trot.

She added her leg too strongly, and he rushed into a canter instead. She took a deep breath and brought him back to a walk, lengthening the reins to let him relax while she attempted to calm her racing thoughts. Her mind was distracted, and her body was tense, so she was giving him unintentional cues. He was doing everything she asked, whether or not it was exactly what she had meant to communicate.

"Sorry, buddy," she said, giving him a pat. She sat tall again and let her attention stray to the way the streaky sunlight was breaking through the clouds and reflecting off the water.

Over the past few days, she had tried to forget about her trip to Seattle and back with Gina, but obviously that wasn't working for her. She owed it to Foam to get her head back in the game before she schooled him anymore, so she tried to untangle the knots forming in her mind and stomach.

Some of the day she'd spent with Gina had been thrilling, as their playful talk had crossed the boundary into flirtation a few times. Neither had seemed to mind the undercurrent of potential that passed between them now and again. Wren certainly didn't, and Gina hadn't shown any signs of backing away. They were both adults, both aware of where they stood with each other as far as the future went. Wren had somehow shifted from thinking she wouldn't mind if her temporary relationship with Gina led to sex, to actively hoping it would. They had different attitudes toward technology—to say the least—but Wren was fairly certain Gina wouldn't bring her computer to bed with them, so it wasn't an issue for her. Despite Gina's jokes the other day about doing Google searches while talking to Wren, her phone had been sitting on her lap untouched during the entire conversation, its screen dark. Even though Gina's life seemed relentlessly entangled in the internet, she was surprisingly capable—and seemingly comfortable—disconnecting from it.

The less appealing part of their afternoon together was obviously the time in the store. The place itself was bad enough, overfilled as it was with technology at its worst—countless screens bombarding the mind relentlessly with speedy images designed to shorten attention spans and destroy brain cells. Adding a discussion about her parents to the already overwhelming experience had been too much.

Wren's stomach clenched at the memory, and Foam jerked his head in the air, faltering to a halt as he tried to interpret what she wanted from him. She forcibly exhaled and loosened her taut muscles, and he started walking again. Having a sensitive, carefully trained high-school dressage horse was an amazing experience, but a challenging one, as well. She couldn't bring anything but her focused best to their rides because he had learned to listen to the tiniest signals from her. A barely visible shift of her weight was often enough to produce an extravagant response.

She tentatively approached the subject in her mind again,

keeping her breathing steady, and Foam continued on without a fuss. Was she angry because Gina was clearly another of her parents' fans? No, she knew they were superstars in the geek world. She would have been surprised if Gina hadn't been familiar with them, but she hadn't expected her to still be using their software. She had assumed the technology was no longer relevant since the original WREN was only a year or so older than she was. Her parents were a bit vague about the timeline of their two creations, one human and one not, and Wren had always suspected she was the result of some WREN-based celebration. She tried to avoid the subject when she was with them because she really didn't want to know any of the details.

Foam tossed his head again. Not unexpectedly, given the direction her thoughts had just taken. She backtracked to the store again in her mind, making sure she got to the root of her tension. Otherwise, she needed to call it a day until she was able to ride without sending mixed signals.

Gina was the daughter her parents would have loved. Wren had no doubt they had expected any child produced by the two of them to be a computer prodigy, and Gina would likely have thrived in their home, as opposed to what sounded like a town full of closed-minded bullies. Oddly enough, Wren almost wished that Gina *had* been her parents' child. Not because she hated them or because she had had a truly awful childhood—neither was true—but because Gina would have been spared a lot of pain and cruelty if she had been raised in their environment.

Gina deserved to be in a place where she was treated with respect and kindness. She was funny, smart, sexy. Thoughtful, too, in the way she had understood Wren's discomfort and sought to make it go away on the trip from the store to her car, and again on the ferry. Wren had enjoyed the convoluted, silly titles for blog posts Gina said she would write for Wren. They had gotten longer and more elaborate as she went, but they all ended with some variation of *scram* or *get the hell off my property*. Wren had been laughing so hard, she had almost failed to realize that Gina was carefully extracting ideas with real potential to be helpful and interesting from Wren's comments. And, damn it, Wren had found herself getting excited about writing down and sharing some of her favorite exercises that had really helped her own students.

Foam halted again and stomped his foot. Wren closed her eyes and sighed, finally seeing what had her tied in knots. Her parents were stressors, but she had spent a lifetime as their daughter, so this wasn't news. The store had been awful, but she had obviously shopped before and had survived the experience. Gina was the wildcard.

Wren looked up as if her eyes had been drawn by a magnet, and saw Gina walking down the slope toward the arena with a camera on a strap around her neck. Grover was at her side, but Biscuit raced over to greet him, and the two stayed under their usual tree while Gina continued into the arena.

Wren was fine with Gina being here on the farm, as much as she complained about it. She liked talking to her, had fun joking with her, and would be excited to have sex with her if they made progress in that direction. What she couldn't handle was having Gina *know* her. To see her upset and understand how to make her feel better. To make what should have been the worst day ever—since it included having a discussion about her parents and their songbird-killing software while in the middle of a store full of computers—one of the most enjoyable afternoons she had spent in a long time. If Wren was going to give in to a relationship she knew was only temporary for the first time in her life, she wished it would be one she didn't care deeply about. One that would be easy to let go when the time came. Gina would leave her wanting more.

Wren nudged Foam into a walk and guided him in Gina's direction. She couldn't tell Gina to leave, and she really didn't want to give up the better parts of having her here. She just needed to be more careful with how much of herself she shared. And while she was at it, she should probably stop encouraging Gina to talk about herself if she didn't volunteer the information up front. They had a fun relationship going, but it didn't need to go too deep, or Wren would be stuck in it forever, long after Gina went back to her city life.

"You're trespassing," she called as Gina walked across the tanbark toward her. "I don't remember giving you permission to enter the arena."

"Can I apply for a temporary visa?"

Wren paused, as if giving the question some thought. "What are you planning to do? Film a Get Ready for Lunch With Me video?"

"That's not a thing. And I'm not here to film myself. I want to take some still pictures of you riding."

Trying to ride was more like it. Wren didn't want a bad schooling day to be recorded for posterity. Or displayed on the internet for hundreds of strangers to see. "I thought you were keeping identifiable pictures off your…your places where you post things."

"I mostly want to take some photos for *your* places where you'll post things," Gina said, shaking her head as she spoke, most likely at Wren's awkward phrasing. "And here's a professional tip. Social media marketing is more effective if your viewers can identify you and your farm."

Wren wrinkled her nose. "I'd prefer to remain a mystery."

"All right. Maybe your viewers will be able to identify the

person who buys this place after you go bankrupt." She spun around and started to walk away.

"Fine," Wren said, and Gina turned back with a grin on her face. Wren waved her hand in a vague gesture. "Click away."

"It's a digital camera. There's no audible click anymore."

"Thank you. That is useful information that deserves to take up space in my brain."

Wren felt a little more at ease since she and Gina had slipped back into their contentious roles of antisocial Wren and computer expert Gina. She felt some of her tension slip away as she asked Foam to trot again. He felt balanced and fluid underneath her, and her relief made her relax even more. She noticed Gina moving around the ring, taking photos, and she spent a few moments wondering why she was standing at such odd angles. Wren was sure her head was going to be chopped off in most of the shots. Eventually, though, she lost herself in her schooling session and merely felt Gina as a comforting presence, without focusing on what she was doing.

After she had ridden Foam through a warm-up and some progressively more difficult exercises, she collected him and asked for more energy at the same time. He was still trotting, but he lifted his knees higher and hesitated for a lengthy beat with every step. Once he had gone along one side of the arena, she released some of the pressure, and he flowed into a regular trot again. She came back to a walk and reached down to hug his neck.

"Wow," Gina said, watching Wren with her camera lowered and resting against her hip. "He looked like he was dancing. What was he doing?"

"It's called *passage*," Wren said. "It's one of the most advanced movements he'll have to do in his career, and it's still fairly new for him. Eventually he'll be strong enough to stay in it longer."

"You both made it seem effortless. It was beautiful." Gina turned her attention to her camera, swiping her thumb across the viewscreen and poking at buttons while Wren walked in a large circle around her. After a few moments Gina looked up again. "Do you want to see the pictures?"

"Yes. Did you take very many? We've only been out here a few minutes."

Gina laughed and shook her head. "I've been watching you for forty-five minutes. I had over a hundred, but not all of them were usable, and I deleted a bunch. It took me several tries to learn how to time my shots with his movement."

Wren halted, and Gina came over to Foam's side. She held the camera between them, resting her elbow on Wren's knee to keep her hand steady. Wren exhaled slowly, feeling Gina's body pressed against her leg and seeing the blond end of a lock of Gina's hair curled against her thigh. She felt her tension return, but it was the good kind this time. The kind that beat in her veins like a quick pulse, pumping anticipation through her body, singing of possibility. Her body had no common sense.

"These first ones are for my Instagram, so they're more abstract. The entire western side of the state can be reached in a day, so I'm planning to travel around and take pictures, sort of a weekend trip travelogue, and these could have been taken in any dressage arena around the state."

Wren leaned forward to see, first lost in the spicy scent of Gina's hair, but then mesmerized by the pictures she had taken. They were only pieces of her and Foam, but they were full of life and movement. One showed merely his fetlocks and hooves as he trotted by one of the black-and-white arena markers. Gina had caught him in the moment when all four hooves were suspended above the ground, so he looked like he was levitating. Another was a picture of them moving away from Gina and toward the bay-side of the arena, with only

Wren's shiny black boot and Foam's gray shoulder set against the blue-gray background, as if they were skimming over the surface of the water.

"These are amazing, Gina," she said, looking at a photo of Foam's hind legs, with his tail swishing to one side. Both ankles were deeply flexed, one on the ground supporting his weight and the other lifted high in *passage*. "I'd love to have some of these enlarged and framed."

Gina patted her on the knee. "Of course. Just buy a computer, and I'll email them to you."

Keep touching me like that, and I'll buy anything you say. "That's blackmail," Wren said out loud, keeping the other thought to herself. "Are you really holding photos as hostages?"

Gina shrugged, apparently not shamed at all. "Look. These are ones we can use for advertising you as a trainer."

Wren admired the next pictures as well, although the previous ones showcased Gina's skills more dynamically. While the others had been tightly focused, these were meant to be expansive. They not only illustrated her riding ability and Foam's level of quality, but they also were carefully angled to show off the farm, with its green paddocks and water view.

"Damn," she said. "Did you have to make the place look this good? People will actually want to come here." She looked around for inspiration. "You know, there's a lot of mud in the western pasture, and the fence behind the barn needs to be repaired. We should post some pictures of those."

Gina lifted her camera before Wren realized what she was doing and took a close-up picture of her. "There," she said, looking at the screen. "I'll post this crotchety face of yours. That'll scare them away."

"Good thinking," Wren said. She slid off Foam's back

without realizing how close she'd be to Gina when she landed. She took a step back and bumped into Foam's side. "Well, I should…um…take him back to the barn."

Gina stood in the center of the arena and watched Wren walk away. She had planned to suggest that they get together soon and talk about the work she needed to do for the farm, make a plan for Wren's social media presence, but Gina had changed her mind at the last minute. After watching Wren ride and then standing so close to her, Gina was too edgy to sit and chat with her.

She looked at the last photo she had taken. Wren's face gazed back at her, with an expression of surprise, since she was just registering what Gina was about to do, tinged with a smile as she asked Gina to take photos of the worst parts of her farm. Like the pictures of Foam's legs, this one had energy and movement flowing through the static photo and bringing it to life. Crotchety was not an apt description of Wren. Drop-dead gorgeous was more accurate.

Gina skimmed through the pictures again as she headed back to the apartment. She was glad she had her camera with her today—she had needed something to occupy her while she watched Wren ride and to keep her from standing in the center of the ring, drooling. Wren was graceful and beautiful on the ground, but she became something else in the saddle. Confident and elegant, with a subtlety that she didn't always possess in conversation. Then, she was raw. Real. More herself than anyone Gina had ever known. While riding, she was a more polished version of that self. The same, but slightly different, like Gina's online and real-world selves.

One thing was certain. These photos of Wren riding were going to prove Gina was right—she was going to be a breeze to market. All Gina needed to do was figure out how to do her job without letting her confusing feelings for Wren get in the way. Her first couple of days had been a lot to handle, with the move and the near-constant exposure to Wren, and she had thought that lying low for another two or three days would give her the distance she needed to regain her composure. Maybe she should have tried for two or three months instead.

She paused in her obsessive flow of thoughts about Wren and realized that the word *months* had unexpectedly not given her the dry heaves when it was applied to her stint here. She was surprised to find she wasn't entirely unhappy in this place, as she had assumed she would be. She was slowly getting used to the constant bird chatter, and she liked having Grover as her bodyguard. Mostly, though, it was Wren, with her jokes and flirtatious remarks, who gave Gina something to think about beyond how much her life had changed and how upset she had been by all the adjustments. Even when she was only watching her ride or work around the farm from a distance, she was somehow comforting and mesmerizing at the same time.

Gina stood in the doorway of the apartment and frowned at the piles of boxes. She was losing sight of her goals here. She had already found herself avoiding some PR opportunities, focusing on the creative side of her career instead of the necessary marketing side. As much as she had complained about being surrounded by nature here on the Peninsula, she felt a sense of relief being away from the stuffy reception rooms, where carrying on stilted conversations and shuffling past displays of merch were part of the ritual. She had also given up her focus on fashioning her living space into something unique and personal. Working on her Seattle apartment had brought a lot of joy into her life—not to mention the significant increase in sponsorships and affiliate links since her home decor and restoration videos and blogs had been among her most popular. She had managed to come up with numerous ways to spend as little money as possible while still creating a sanctuary out of a plain apartment. Even though her old place had been spottily redecorated, she had been working toward the goal of a complete and cohesive space. Without making the decision consciously, she had given up on that aspect of her online business, choosing instead to focus on ideas like local photo stories and her chattier types of videos. This apartment was shelter, and nothing more. She hadn't wanted to fully acknowledge that she was here to stay, at least for a while.

She walked from one end of the apartment to the other— admittedly a short jaunt—with Grover sticking close to her. She tried to keep her new perspective, the one that could face potential months here without wanting to curl in a ball and cry. The room was tiny, but that meant she could conceivably redo the entire place without much cost. Surely she could reach followers who were on extremely tight budgets and who lived in apartments and homes that were far from fancy. She needed to make this period of her life more profitable   creatively and financially—and not lose sight of the motivation she needed to push herself. Comfort zones were dangerous things.

Gina set her camera on the table. She needed to do this for her career, if nothing else. Too much had been taken away, and she couldn't let her content stagnate. She had to work with what she had and turn it into something special.

She had been merely existing in this room since she had arrived. Truly living here and making the place her own, even if for a short time, had at first meant she was giving up and accepting her exile. Well, she *had* started to accept it, but a new issue had arisen to make her fight to continue seeing herself as an outsider here. Wren. Gina could turn the apartment into an adorable showroom-quality space and still walk away from it without a second glance as soon as she got the chance. If she let herself get too attached to Wren, though, she might be tempted to put off her return to the city, compromising on her dreams. She could afford to buy some paint and cheap old furniture to put her mark on this apartment, but she couldn't afford to get attached to this farm and its inhabitants in any way beyond superficial.

Their time together in the computer and grocery stores had been fun but disconcerting. There had been a lot of sharing, on both sides, and Gina wasn't sure how she felt about it. Her life had been turned upside down, and while she needed to make the best of it for her work, she didn't need a personal and romantic entanglement to confuse matters even more. She was already relaxing into this life, even after such a short time. Filming and creating content, sparring with Wren. Avoiding cold calls, PR events, and networking. When those opportunities had been just outside her door, just in the neighborhood beyond her own, she had managed to overcome her natural inclination to crawl inside her shell and had pushed her limits. Somehow, adding the ferry trip across the Sound had given her a built-in excuse to slow down her marketing drive. Even missing one or two events could mean months of trying to catch up again. If she fell too far behind, she'd never reach her goals.

She would force herself back into the marketing hustle, no matter how much time she had to spend waiting in line for ferries. Tomorrow. Today, she would start with a renewed interest in renovating her apartment, hopefully giving herself some sense of control over her physical space when she had so little in other areas of her life.

She picked up the camera again and swiped back to the picture of Wren. No, she didn't need romance in her life, or any sort of emotional ties. Sex, though? Inadvisable, she decided, turning off her camera so the screen went black. That meant continuing to avoid Wren, and not giving in to the nagging desire to ask Wren to accompany her to Poulsbo to look for furnishings for the apartment.

And hoping desperately that if she *did* ask, Wren would have sense enough to turn her down.

Chapter Eleven

Well, neither one of them had any sense. Gina hadn't managed to walk from her apartment to the car without stopping to ask Wren if she wanted to join her, and Wren hadn't even hesitated before agreeing to the trip. Despite Gina's repeated vow to put distance between them, here they were, back in close quarters in her car.

The drive around the edge of Liberty Bay into Poulsbo was a quick one, and Gina followed Wren's directions off the highway only moments after she had gotten on it. She passed the small but more civilized edge of Poulsbo—with its fast-food restaurants, predictable strip-mall-type stores, and larger grocery chains—without much more than a single longing glance, only putting up a protest when Wren told her to keep driving even past the older downtown area. She had expected them to head down the hill into the more touristy part of Poulsbo, but Wren shook her head and pointed forward.

"I wanted to buy some furniture to restore, not cut down trees and make my own," Gina complained as they left even the most rudimentary signs of city life behind.

"You said you wanted to show people how to redecorate on a budget. You won't find anything inexpensive in an antique store in downtown Poulsbo. The prices there will be even higher than you'd find in Seattle."

Gina grew more convinced that she'd rather pay exorbitant prices than continue driving past the middle of nowhere. She was about to turn around despite Wren's insistence that she continue when Wren pointed at a faded wooden sign tacked on a tree.

"Antiques," Gina read, steering down the rutted gravel road. "Is it referring to what they sell, or to the people who live down here?"

"Trust me, you'll love this place," Wren said, seemingly unfazed by Gina's sarcasm.

"Of course I trust you. Even though that's exactly the kind of sign I'd post if I was a serial killer trying to lure stupid city folk to my out-of-the-way lair."

"Very funny. Meanwhile, I'm mentally rehearsing where I'll put the emphasis when I say *I told you so.*"

Wren started a quiet chant of the phrase, changing her inflection to a different word each time. Gina was about to punch her in the arm to make her stop when she rounded a bend and saw a huge barn ahead of her. The paint was chipping so much the color was barely discernible, but the yard around it was filled with ancient farm implements. Any one of them would have looked great in a garden, twined with flowering plants.

Gina exhaled audibly. "This is so cool. Go ahead, you can say it now."

Wren cleared her throat as if preparing to take the stage. "I *told* you so."

"Good choice," Gina said with a nod. She grinned at Wren, letting go of her reservations about bringing her along. Only because Wren was proving to be useful in today's search, of course, and not at all because she was just plain fun to be around. "Come on. I can't wait to see what's inside."

If Gina had thought the outside of the place looked

cluttered, it was nothing compared to what awaited her inside the barn. She paused beyond the doorway, letting her eyes adjust to the dim lighting. This was the perfect type of antique store for her bargain-hunting venture. The entire barn had been gutted so it was one huge room filled with rows of folding tables that looked ready to buckle under the weight of their loads. Each was piled high with dusty items, randomly assorted as if no thought at all had gone into their placement. There were no sections for china or jewelry or old toys— everything was thrown together in the kind of free-for-all that meant trash and treasures were equally likely to be found. Gina felt the thrill of an impending hunt shiver through her.

"Are you all right?" Wren asked, putting her hand on Gina's upper back, probably preparing to catch her if she toppled over. Wren pointed at a threadbare red velvet sofa near the entrance. "Do you need a lie-down before we go all the way inside?"

Gina laughed and fanned herself with her hand. "I do feel like I'm about to swoon," she said, still gazing around the large space. The chinks in the walls let in glittering sprinkles of sunlight. "This place is amazing. Do you realize how much great stuff we're going to find here?"

Wren looked around with decidedly less enthusiasm in her expression than Gina felt. "If you say so. I fail to see how any of this dirty junk is going to actually improve the apartment, but you asked me to lead you to cheap old stuff." She waved her arms with a flourish. "Ta-da!"

Gina shook her head, leading them down the first row of tables. "I thought you were all about preserving the past and honoring traditions. I'd expect this to be exactly your type of store."

Wren picked up a single sock that might have been yellow under all its grime. She held it gingerly by her fingertips. "I'm all about preserving time-honored traditions and high-quality artisanal items, not random trash."

"Yuck. Put that down. We're not here to buy clothes," Gina said. She swatted at Wren to make her drop the sock, but instead of pulling away after, she gripped Wren's hand. "Ooh, look. This is more like it."

Gina pulled Wren farther down the aisle before stopping suddenly and letting go of her hand. Wren's momentum carried her into Gina's space, and she came to a halt pressed close to Gina's side. Gina nearly forgot what she had been so excited about mere seconds before. She reached out and extracted a small wooden chest from under some tangled Christmas tree lights, trying to ignore the way her body responded to Wren's with a rush of warmth. The feeling was overwhelming, but Gina didn't move away.

"Do you need a dresser for your dolly's clothes?" Wren asked, her breath brushing across Gina's neck, making her hair sway and fanning the heat inside her. The contrast between Wren's teasing voice and the erotic sensation she was causing was intoxicating. Gina had never realized that playful conversations could feel like foreplay.

She shook her head, focusing with effort on the object she was holding. She opened each of the three doors one at a time. "No, but can't you picture this with some little pots of herbs in it? It'll be adorbs."

"Adorbs?" Wren repeated, with a tinge of disbelief in her voice. "Is that somehow supposed to mean adorable?"

"Obvi," Gina said, rolling her eyes in an exaggerated way and trying not to laugh. Wren was too predictable. "It's a cuter word and it's more efficient."

Wren took a step back and looked at her as if she was as incomprehensible as the bank of televisions in Best Buy. "It saved two syllables. What are you going to do with all that extra time?"

Gina shrugged. She missed feeling Wren's closeness, but at least her mind could return to normal functioning now that they weren't touching. Or at least semi-normal since Wren hadn't moved very far away. "If I use enough of them during the day, I'll have time to send an extra text or two."

Wren shook her head. "Meanwhile words become plastic water bottles, tossed in the landfill that is the internet."

"That's a bit dramatic." Gina patted Wren on the shoulder before turning away and continuing along the row. She couldn't look at Wren and keep a straight face, so she spoke without looking back. "Don't worry—you'll adapt. We just need to get you caught up on the kind of language you'll have to use on your social media platforms."

She heard silence, then Wren's footsteps as she jogged to catch up. "I can't imagine any scenario in which I'd need to use the word *adorbs*," she said as soon as she got close to Gina again.

Gina waved her hand as if to shush her. "Whatevs. As long as I'm posting your content, your blog is going to be littered with slang. You want correct English, learn how to use the computer."

"You're kidding. Are you kidding? I can't tell."

Gina couldn't keep from laughing at Wren's plaintive tone. She faced her again. "Of course I'm kidding. Do you really think I'm going to write about how adorbs Foam is when he canters on the correct lead?" She stopped laughing and assumed what she hoped was a menacing expression as she pointed at Wren's chest in warning. "Never forget, though, that I am capable of doing it. You'll never know for sure what I'm posting, so eventually you'll have to be able to do it yourself."

"You have a sick sense of humor," Wren said as they continued walking. "I love it."

❖

Wren carefully packed each item in the trunk of the car as Gina handed them to her. Gina insisted on calling them treasures, but Wren pictured quotation marks around the word in her mind. Gina would probably surprise her with the finished products, earning the right to say her own *I told you so.*

Wren slid into the passenger seat and directed Gina as they made their way back to Poulsbo and to Wren's favorite café. She really should be back at the farm right now, riding the two training horses she had meant to school after Foam. Ever since she had dismounted in the arena and found herself nearly on top of Gina, she had been reaffirming her need to stay away from her barn's temporary tenant. Then, at the first mention of a trip to town together, Wren had tossed out all her carefully crafted reasoning and agreed to go. She had tried to convince herself that she needed to go in order to help Gina find the store, but her logic didn't hold up any better than it had when she had gone with Gina to Scandia's grocery store, especially given the few options for getting lost in the area. She didn't actually need to be in the car to tell Gina to drive for two miles and turn left.

She really had no excuse besides how much she liked being with Gina, even though she had a mean streak where Wren's resistance to using a computer was concerned, first holding her photos hostage, and then threatening to make Wren sound like an inane schoolgirl if she didn't write and post her own stuff. Still, Wren had a hard time caring about those threats when she was near enough to smell the honeyed sweetness of Gina's hair and see the silky strands moved by

Wren's breath when she spoke with her mouth barely an inch away from Gina's neck.

So she'd spend the afternoon with Gina, getting back in time to teach her evening lessons. And she'd turn on the tall lights surrounding her outdoor arena and exercise her horses when they were done. Just for the chance to get close to her again.

"Impressive parallel parking," she said, shutting her car door and joining Gina on the sidewalk. Wren avoided the rare good spots along Poulsbo's main street since her truck was awkward to maneuver, but Gina had wedged her car into a prime place with only a foot to spare.

"It's a city skill," Gina said. "I can park even faster if I think someone else is eying my spot."

Wren smiled and opened the door of the tearoom. She started to walk inside, only to have her path blocked by a woman who grabbed her into a tight hug.

"Hi, Annie," Wren said, her voice slightly muffled since she was squashed against Annie's bosom.

"Where have you been?" she asked, releasing Wren and putting her hands on her hips. "Shame on you for not coming by sooner."

"I know, I'm sorry. It's been busy at the farm." Wren gestured behind Annie. "This is my friend Gina. Gina, this is Anneke. She's the owner and chef here."

"Nice to meet…oh, okay…" Gina had put her hand out to shake but was swept into a hug instead.

"So this is what you meant by busy," Annie said, elbowing Wren hard enough to send her several feet to one side. "Bring your cute new girlfriend and come along. I have a nice quiet table for you by the kitchen."

Wren knew from experience that no table within reach of Annie's kitchen could ever be considered *quiet*. She didn't bother protesting that Gina wasn't her girlfriend since Annie was already halfway across the room.

"Sorry about the hug," she said to Gina as they trailed behind. "I should have warned you."

"No big deal," Gina said, rubbing her side. "What are a few broken ribs?"

She was smiling, though, and didn't seem bothered by the unconventional greeting, even though Wren doubted she was hugged by many restaurant owners in Seattle. After they were seated, Wren busied herself looking at the menu even though she knew it by heart. "Sorry about the girlfriend part, too. I'll tell her we're just…well, friends." She tried to keep her voice even, but heard a slight rising inflection at the end, as if she was asking Gina where they stood.

"Don't bother," Gina said with a shrug. Wren looked up, but Gina was now the one staring fixedly at her menu. "I doubt she'll believe you, anyway. And it's not like I'll be here long enough for it to matter."

Wren let Gina's words settle into her mind while they talked about food choices and gave their orders. Taken at face value, it was an innocent conversation. When Wren dug a little deeper, though, she thought she might be reading something else into it. A hint of possibility, maybe? An invitation to play a part for a short time? She wasn't sure if that's how Gina meant her words to be interpreted, and she also didn't know if she would be able to remain disconnected enough to let Gina go without any emotional repercussions.

"So, what exactly did she mean by *new* girlfriend?" Gina asked, looking at Wren again with a teasing smile. "New, as in *the latest in a long line of* or new, as in *wow, this is new since she's never brought a girlfriend here before.*"

"Somewhere in the middle," Wren answered truthfully. "I guess my approach to dating is consistent with the rest of my life. I don't like disposable relationships, but I also won't remain in them if they aren't going anywhere meaningful. I tend to make my mind up quickly whether something is worth my time and effort."

"Brutal, but honest," Gina said. She fiddled with her place setting, avoiding eye contact again. "So you'd never accept a relationship without a serious future?"

"I never have before," Wren said. "Then again, I've never met anyone who's tempted me to try. I suppose someday... given the right circumstances...I might change my mind."

This earned her a burst of Gina's musical laughter, which made Wren smile. "You? Change your mind? I don't believe it."

Wren didn't know if either of them was ready to make any decisions about their relationship yet, and she felt a sense of relief when Gina's playful words eased the serious tone of their conversation. Once their sandwiches arrived, she steered the discussion back to the more neutral topic of Gina's plans for the junk she had bought.

"I've seen the apartment, you know. I can't imagine a few decorative touches will turn it into anything close to your last place. It was as beautiful as anything I've seen in magazines," she said, wrapping her hands around the thick slabs of homemade bread surrounding her tempeh, lettuce, and tomato sandwich and taking a bite.

Gina looked at her in surprise. "You've seen my posts?"

Wren shook her head. "Your portfolio. I looked through it while I was on the phone with Dianna, yelling at her for sending you for an interview."

Gina picked up a wedge of avocado that had fallen out of her overstuffed sandwich and ate it. "Ah, yes. The fateful day of the interview. You were charming, by the way."

"Was I?" Wren asked, feigning innocence. "Funny. I was

going for unwelcoming, but I suppose my natural charisma seeped through somehow."

Gina laughed. "A good dose of smart-ass seeped through, too. But back to the apartment, I'm sure there are plenty of people who are trying to make the best of a similar situation. They'll be amazed how a well-placed display of herbs can distract the eye from swarms of flies and spiders."

Wren laughed, hoping Gina was kidding. She had gotten rid of a lot of spiders when she cleaned the place, but more might have moved in since then. "Are you going to embed the words *save me* in the title of the blog?"

Gina rolled her eyes. "I think the need for rescue will be implied once I post the before photos." She took a drink of water and her expression turned more thoughtful. "I'm thinking of a title like 'From Cobwebbed to Cozy: Transforming the Unconventional Living Space.'"

"Oh," Wren said, setting her sandwich back on her plate. "That actually sounds really good."

They spent the rest of their lunch talking about Gina's plans for the apartment. Wren listened and asked questions, but part of her mind was spinning off onto tangents. Gina was funny and creative and smart—even discussing a seemingly neutral topic with her made Wren want more, want to be closer and get to know her better. She heard the sentences they were speaking and the background noise of the busy restaurant, but the word *girlfriend* still hovered in the air, threatening to drown out everything else.

CHAPTER TWELVE

C oming through. Get ready to edit me out."
"You don't need to tell me that every time you walk by," Gina said as she adjusted her tripod and peered through the camera's viewfinder. "Trust me, whenever I see your face on the screen, I edit you out."

Gina had edited Wren out of the videos but hadn't deleted the footage yet because some of it might be useful for Wren's posts—if she ever made any. Most wasn't, but Gina always hesitated when her finger hovered over the delete icon. She had chosen the path of denial, though, and refused to examine why she kept any of it.

She heard an unfamiliar laugh and looked up from the camera. Wren was standing in the doorway, breathtaking as always in her tight riding pants and tall boots, and a petite woman was next to her, holding the reins of an equally tiny brown mare.

"I'm Dianna," she said, leaning forward to shake hands. "And you must be Gina. It's nice to finally meet you in person."

"You, too," Gina said. Ah, the accountant. She hoped Dianna wouldn't ask for some sort of progress report since she and Wren hadn't done any work together yet. As if by mutual agreement, they had kept a casual distance from each other since their antique hunting. Gina had accepted every invitation to go to Seattle for business that came her way, and Wren was busy getting ready for her show, which was lucky since they seemed only able to handle short doses in each other's company—not because they couldn't stand any more than that but because they wanted more. Gina did, at least. She thought Wren did as well, but she wasn't sure. Wren always asked about her projects if she was filming or taking photos, and Gina had learned about most of the horses as Wren passed by on her way to ride them. They hadn't had any lengthy one-on-one time, though, let alone making time for discussing Wren's social media opportunities. "Are you here for a lesson?"

"I am," Dianna said, giving her horse a pat on the neck. She smiled with a sweet expression at Gina, then at Wren. "It's so nice of Wren to fit me in even though she's so busy with all her new clients."

She made a show of scanning the deserted farm. "Oh, wait. I don't see *any* new clients. The two of you are working on fixing that, aren't you?"

Gina felt as if she had been called to the principal's office. She fought the urge to mumble *yes, ma'am* and decided she was never again thinking the word *sweet* in association with Dianna. Fierce was more like it.

"I'm busier in the afternoons," Wren said. "Gina likes to film out here in the mornings, so I usually try to keep it quiet for her."

"Hey!" Gina glared at Wren. Way to throw her under the bus. Afternoons were, if anything, quieter than the peaceful mornings at this farm. Wren gave her a pleading look, though, and Gina shut her mouth instead of protesting. She wasn't here for long, but Wren would have to face her accountant regularly in the future. She'd take the fall just this once. "She's right," Gina said. "I'm kind of a prima donna about having a quiet set."

Dianna rolled her eyes. "Please. I know Wren is to blame. She's afraid that if she looks at a computer screen it'll steal her soul."

"Hey!" Wren echoed.

Dianna turned to face Gina again. "But you're the professional. It's your job to get her on board with this."

"We went to a computer store," Wren said.

Gina nodded. "And discussed software."

"And bought the internet."

Gina laughed. "We bought access to the internet. A mobile hotspot."

"It cost enough," Wren said, smiling back at her. "We should have gotten the whole internet for what we paid."

Dianna looked back and forth between them and shook her head. Gina had a feeling she was seeing several layers beneath the surface of her interchange with Wren. "Hm. All right, just make sure *some* work is being done around here."

"It's a process," Gina said. She remembered what Dianna had told her about Wren's expenses and the risk of losing this place if she didn't increase her income. She had been so focused on her discomfiting attraction to Wren that she had been all too willing to let Wren's lack of enthusiasm for the project keep them from getting started.

"I understand it will take time. But you've at least developed a marketing plan, haven't you? With stepped goals and set dates for accomplishing them?" She turned to Wren and pointed a threatening finger at her. "And by set dates, I mean actual days this month, not something like when hell freezes over."

Dianna put on her riding helmet and tucked her hair neatly inside. "I am going to take Pixie to the arena and start warming up while the two of you make an appointment to meet and discuss your plans. Today. That's a darling little cabinet, Gina."

She switched gears—and tone of voice—so quickly, Gina took a moment to catch up and remember what she was about to film. She had the small three-drawer chest from her trip with Wren balanced on the bucket-table.

"She's mean," Wren said once they were alone.

"But she's right. I'm sorry I haven't been pushing you more."

Wren waved off her apology with a grin. "Don't even blame yourself. We both know she's right, and I'm the one at fault. So let's get this over with. Would eleven be okay?"

Gina nodded. She had already made some preliminary notes about the directions she thought Wren could take, so she didn't need time to prepare. "I'll meet you in your office?"

"That'll work." She glanced down and frowned at Grover. "I believe my dog was white when I loaned him to you. Why is he green now?"

Gina looked at Grover, who had green flecks of paint along his cheek and neck. She was relieved to see him lying on his left side, which was covered with a wide swath of wood stain, so it was hidden from view. "Oh. Well, I've been doing some painting in the apartment. You said you didn't mind if I made a few changes, remember?"

"Please. Unless you're taking a sledgehammer to the walls, I don't see how you could make the place look worse."

"Thanks, and I promise he'll be white again when you get him back." She might have to shave off the paint and stain, but he had plenty of fur. No one would miss a few handfuls.

"White and fluffy," Wren warned, as if anticipating Gina's solution to the paint problem.

Gina waved her off. "Go teach your lesson and stop worrying. He'll almost certainly still have some fluff."

❖

Gina half expected Wren to come up with some excuse to miss their meeting, but Gina saw her moving around in the office when she came down from her apartment with paper and notebooks stacked on top of her laptop. Gina had considered backing out herself, but for different reasons. Wren simply didn't want to be here, in close proximity to a computer. Gina, on the other hand, was afraid of what she might say or learn if they let the conversation stray beyond the confines of Wren's work. The subject of computers was a trigger for both of them. They represented an escape for Gina, a way out of the miserable, hateful town where she had grown up. She still wasn't sure about the details of Wren's childhood, but she guessed that her parents' computer work had somehow alienated Wren from them. Either way, once the hot-button topic came up, she and Wren crossed lines of intimacy that Gina wanted to reinforce—not break down. Physical intimacy was something she maybe wouldn't mind sharing with Wren, just as long as the emotional side of things didn't come as part of the package.

Gina had tried sharing parts of herself with friends in school, but they had turned on her, using the information she had given them as an entry fee to join the more popular, powerful groups of kids in their class. Her sexuality, the imagined worlds she created in her mind based on favorite books, her distaste for the way some of the students treated animals or unpopular kids. All of them became fuel to feed the animosity that was directed at her for no other reason than she was different. Her parents hadn't been much help, since they basically told her to conform, to make an effort to fit in. So she had shut down. Her dreams of medieval fantasy worlds changed until her image of utopia became a big city, where so many people were different that one more wouldn't be noticed. Where strangers barely noticed her on the street, friends were carefully kept behind a screen, and where her infrequent romantic flirtations could be confined to people on the other side of the country or even the world.

Wren threatened the anonymity she had carefully cultivated. And, in turn, she shared enough about her own past to embed herself in Gina's mind as a three-dimensional, complex friend. Someone who couldn't be blocked from her thoughts without regret when she went back to Seattle. Oddly enough, Gina thought a physical relationship with Wren would give her more of a sense of distance. A temporary tryst with Wren while she was waiting out her term in Poulsbo was something Gina could easily classify and understand. There were clear rules for that sort of relationship, and even though Gina wasn't in the habit of having casual flings, she knew what to expect.

A more romantic relationship—with their lifestyles, passions, and values coming into play—was definitely not as clear cut and would become messy once Gina was able to move back to some version of her old life.

She took a deep breath and walked through the office's open door. "Oh, you cleaned. It looks nice."

Wren laughed. "Well, I wiped off the chairs and shoved everything that was on top of the desk into one of the drawers." She put her hands on her hips and looked around. "Now that you mention it, it is a pretty big deal. Let's call it our action step for the day."

Wren started toward the door, but Gina grabbed her elbow and pointed at the newly cleaned folding chair. "Ha! Now sit."

Wren flopped onto the chair with a sigh, and Gina pulled the rolling chair closer to the desk and sat down with much less attitude. She set the stack of paper to one side and opened her laptop.

"This is a laptop computer," she said. "This part is the

screen, and this is the keyboard. The keyboard is like a fancy typewriter." She glanced at Wren and bit her lip. "You look confused, so let me break it down a little more. A typewriter is like a fancy pencil. You know what a pencil is, don't you?"

"I think so. Is a pencil a fancy version of the stick I use to draw in the dirt?"

"Very good, Wren," she said, patting her on the knee.

Wren swatted her hand away, but caught it again as Gina was pulling it back and gave her a squeeze before letting go and leaning her elbow on the desk.

"Okay, I think we can assume I know the basics since I was taught to play games on a computer before I could walk and had to do my homework on them until I rebelled in junior high. As long as they haven't changed much in the past twenty years or so, I'm good."

"Computer technology changed in the time it took you to tell that story," Gina said. She opened her browser and navigated to one of her websites. "I thought I'd show you some of the platforms I use, and then we'll decide what will be most effective for your barn."

"Fine. Is a platform like a fancy diving board?"

Gina laughed. "I'm not answering that because you're just trying to distract me. Now look, this is a blog. This would be a good place to start for you since it's about as easy as it gets. You write a few paragraphs about whatever dressage or training topic you want and then post it here. You can add pictures, or links to other websites, if you want. Photos are always a good idea. Remember to think of the computer as primarily a visual medium, not a written one."

"Got it," Wren said.

Gina doubted it, because she could feel Wren's attention wandering as if it was a physical current pulling her away from the computer. She was sitting at an angle to Gina, with her knee lightly pressed against Gina's thigh. Her chin was resting in her hand, propped on the desk, and Gina knew Wren was watching her rather than the screen. She didn't want to complain, since the sensation of being watched by her was close to a caress, but she knew they needed to at least make a start on their project.

She leaned back in the chair suddenly and caught Wren staring at her. "I don't get it," she said, tapping her short nails against the laptop's edge. She had wanted to keep their meeting focused on the nuts and bolts of creating a website or Instagram account, yet here she was delving back into Wren's personal life. She couldn't help it, though. Unless she understood why Wren fought every step, she wouldn't be able to find a way to convince her to try something new. And, admittedly, she was curious about Wren in a way she rarely felt about other people. A dangerous way, but also an irresistible one.

"What don't you get?" Wren put her foot on one of Gina's chair's roller feet and pushed it gently. "Why I don't like technology?"

"No, I think I sort of understand where you're coming from. I've met a few super-genius computer programmers and software designers, and even though I respect them and think they've created amazing things, I would imagine that having some of them as parents or partners would be very lonely." Gina paused, and Wren nodded slightly, as if encouraging her to continue. She was keeping her expression blank, though, and Gina wasn't certain if she was way off base or hitting too close to home. "Maybe a child who was raised in a home where love and attention were complicated things that weren't given freely to her would feel sort of resentful of the object that *did* receive those two things in abundance. Maybe she would grow up and decide to build a simpler life, where she could pretend the computers her parents adored didn't even exist."

Wren watched her in silence for so long that Gina shifted in her chair. "But what do I know? Just a few days ago I was sure you had been raised on a hippie commune."

Wren reached over and traced her thumb over Gina's lips, her fingers trailing down Gina's cheek as she let her hand fall back into her lap. Her touch had been gentle, barely there, but the unexpectedness of it made Gina part her lips as she inhaled, just managing to keep the movement of her breath quiet and not gasp aloud. The burn of Wren's touch lingered even after her hand was gone.

"Sibling rivalry, huh? I'm jealous of my older sister, WREN the first, so I banished her and all her high-tech friends from my kingdom?"

Gina clenched her hands together to keep from reaching up to touch her face, where Wren's fingers had been. She was certain she had some sort of mark seared across her skin. She tried a smile. "Well, that would make you Wren 2.0, the perfected product. The other WREN is the buggy beta version."

Wren gave a snort of laughter. "Until the falcon comes along and eats both of us."

"I was hoping you wouldn't bring up Falcon," Gina said with a playful wince. "It kind of ruins my analogy."

Wren sat back in her chair and crossed her arms over her chest. "I think you're partly right," she said. "But I'm being truer to myself living like I do, so my lifestyle is not so much reactionary as it is a result of who I am. I was always tactile and not theoretical, preferring to write in the dirt with sticks rather than to compose computer code in my head. I liked routines and traditions, solid ideas I could predict, rather than the jarring world of newer versions and constant updates. My parents love me, but they never understood me. They always understood WREN."

"Well, yes," Gina said. "But that's because they created her. I mean, *it*."

Wren spread her hands wide. "They created me, too."

They were quiet for a moment, and Gina thought back to some of the conversations between Wren and her students she had heard over the past few days. "That's why you're drawn to dressage, isn't it? Because of the history and traditions?"

Wren rubbed her hand over the back of her neck. "Yes. It's fascinating. And the sport has evolved over time, but not quickly." She laughed. "You've overheard some of my lessons, I suppose? I could talk about dressage theories all day, so I have to mentally time myself when I start one of my lectures. Some of my riders believe my internal clock is a faulty piece of tech, though."

Gina grinned, pouncing on the opening she'd been waiting for. She had been working in the wrong direction, she realized, by trying to get Wren excited about social media, and then showing her how she could use it to share her passion for horses. She had needed to go the other way, instead, and get Wren fired up about dressage first.

"You wouldn't have a time limit on a blog," she said, leaning toward Wren as if she could channel her own enthusiasm through their legs, where they had been in contact since they had sat down. "You wouldn't have to stop yourself from writing about any topic you choose, because you'll find an audience somewhere, anywhere. You already have your niche—you just need to reach people who want to read what you write. Then they'll comment on your posts, and you'll respond. You'll be having a conversation, not giving a lecture, with people from all over the world."

Wren gave her a pained expression. "All over the world?

I thought I was doing this to get six or seven new students, not to chat with people who will never come here for a lesson."

"Dianna said at least ten. And trust me, you'll get those, too, but you can only handle a finite number of new students, can't you? On social media, you can reach hundreds of people. Thousands. If you're monetizing your blog and your Instagram account, you can make some extra money without having as many people actually come to the farm."

Wren sat forward and poked her finger at the computer, nudging it a fraction of an inch across the desk. "You can make money just by writing blogs? What about posting those face cream videos?"

Gina shoved at Wren's knee, just not hard enough to break their contact. "It's not just about the stupid face cream...Oh, never mind. Yes, and yes. I make money from both. How did you think I made my living, anyway?"

Wren shrugged. "I knew you did this professionally, but I thought of that more as an indication of the amount of time and energy you put into it. Somehow that didn't translate into making money in my mind. I thought maybe you were independently wealthy."

"Yes, that's why I'm living in a glorified stall." Gina paused and considered the state of the apartment when she had first seen it. "Not even glorified. Just one that's on the second story, which I suppose might qualify it as the barn's penthouse apartment." She hesitated for a moment, aware of how unique and very Wren-like Wren's comment about Gina's profession really was. She focused on the value Gina brought to her work, not the dollar signs of what she took away from it.

"It's a challenge, since I never have a set paycheck," Gina said, wanting Wren to understand how seriously she took her career. "The money I make depends on the effort I make to market my sites, and it comes down to numbers, like how many people click on my affiliate links or buy sponsored products I've reviewed. And I only get those sponsorships and ads and things if I have enough people viewing my posts or commenting on my photos or liking my videos. It's much easier to network when I'm close to the stores and businesses that will pay to have me showcase their products or make space for their ads. Which is why it's been hard for me to be here, where I sometimes feel like I've been pushed outside the circle of influencers and revenue sources."

Wren was watching her with a slight frown. "I didn't realize...I guess I thought the great thing about your career was that you could do it from anywhere, as long as you had internet access."

"Well, that's true, in a way," Gina said, suddenly wanting to shift the conversation away from her own experiences. She really *could* do her job from anywhere—it was just easier to make herself join the networking grind when she was too close to have distance or time as an excuse for staying away. And plenty of influencers lived in out-of-the-way or unusual places, but they were the big names, the ones who had reached the kinds of numbers still beyond Gina's grasp. She switched back to talking about Wren—after all, they were here to discuss her social media goals, not Gina's.

"Anyway, back to you," she said. "Even though you need to attract some new clients and potentially monetize one or more of your platforms, you probably aren't going to be driving toward really high numbers of followers, so you're free to focus on what you enjoy. You could do a version of a Get Ready with Me, but you'd be getting ready for a show or just a regular ride. You could talk about grooming tips or your opinion on saddles, or whatever. And if you aren't comfortable doing videos, you can stick with writing or taking pictures. You probably won't make enough to avoid having any students at your farm, but I don't believe that's what you really want, no matter how often you say it. You'd have the potential to make some extra cash, though, from ads and corporate sponsorships. You can be an affiliate for a company and make a percentage of sales that result from your posts, or maybe get some free products in exchange for writing a review."

"Ooh. Barter." Wren sounded happier at the prospect of swapping a review for some sort of horse thing than she had about the money.

Value, not dollar signs. Gina made one last appeal to Wren, using similar language as Wren had used just moments ago, when she had made Gina feel special because of what she personally brought to her job. "You have a unique perspective on the sport, and you're obviously passionate about it. It'd be a shame not to share your ideas with other people, especially those who will value them. Plus, prospective clients will learn about who you are and what you have to offer. You'll not only bring in more students, but they'll be ones who will be likely to fit in well with your program."

Or they'd be women who liked the photos of Wren in sexy, stretchy pants enough to pay for lessons. Gina didn't want to think too much about them.

"All right," Wren said. "I'll give it a try. Just a try, and if I feel like my quality of life is being negatively impacted by this, then I'm done. Fair enough?"

Gina nodded. She had expected a lot more kicking and screaming, so she was going to count this as a major win. "I'd expect nothing less from you," she said. "Start by making a list of some topics you'd like to cover, like we were doing on the ferry, but without the stay-away vibes, and we can use those to fine-tune the tone and theme of your blog. Then we can start to work on creating posts."

"And there won't be a falcon involved?"

Gina bit her lip. Wren wouldn't know the difference if she lied, but she stuck with a vague reassurance instead. "If there is, I'll take care of it. You won't even have to be close enough to see its beady little eyes watching you."

Wren tilted her head back and covered her face with her hands. Then she ran her fingers through her hair and sat up straight again. "Okay. Let's do this. I'll make my list after I teach my next lesson."

Gina snapped her laptop closed and stood up. Wren got up at the same time and took one step toward her, holding herself still and just on the edge of making contact, as if giving Gina a chance to move away if she chose. Gina felt the edge of the desk behind her, pressing against her thighs. Wren in front, but not touching her. Close enough that if Gina bent her knees or pushed her hips forward or even took a deep breath, their bodies would meet.

Wren merely watched her for several long moments, wearing the same trying-to-figure-her-out expression she often seemed to have on her face when she was around Gina. She raised her left hand and drew her index finger over the hair framing Gina's face, shifting her gaze so she was looking at her hand as she separated a lock of hair from the rest with her finger.

Gina couldn't see Wren's hand, but she felt every slight tug and twist, as if her strands of hair had nerve endings like skin, as Wren slowly coiled the lock around her finger. Gina felt her insides coiling in response, until her body was too taut to take more than shallow breaths. Finally, after excruciatingly drawn-out seconds, Wren lowered her hand until the curl of hair slipped off her finger and bounced back into place. Gina blinked as she felt it brush against her cheek. Wren brought her eyes back to meet Gina's, and a smile spread across her face, as slowly as her hand had been moving through Gina's hair.

Gina had been stunned into immobility while Wren first touched her, but now she felt the tension she had been feeling melt into the kind of wanting that wasn't going to sit still and wait any longer. She lifted her hands from where they had been gripping the edge of the desk and settled them on Wren's hip bones, curling her fingers and pulling Wren's body flush against hers. The immediate sensation of her hips and breasts fitting against Wren's as if they had been designed to mesh together made her close her eyes and release her breath in a quiet groan of pleasure. She heard a similar sound echoed from Wren, and she laughed and opened her eyes to see Wren smiling back at her.

Wren put her palms against Gina's cheeks, leaning forward to press her lips against Gina's in a kiss that bypassed tentative and went directly to hungry. She slid her hands back, tangling them in Gina's hair and pulling her closer, deeper into the kiss. Gina tightened her hold, too, meeting Wren's tongue with hers as she felt Wren's thigh ease between her legs, pressing her more firmly against the desk.

In the next moment, Wren stepped away, so suddenly that Gina almost slipped off the desk. Wren reached out a hand to steady her.

"People," she said, waving toward the parking area with her other hand. She moved to the other side of the office and closed her eyes, pinching the bridge of her nose as if struggling to get her thoughts under control. Gina knew exactly how she felt.

Wren exhaled slowly and opened her eyes. "Eric and his mom. He's my one o'clock lesson. Now do you understand why I don't want more people coming here?"

Gina nodded, clearing her throat before she spoke and hoping her voice would manage to work. "You've converted me. And to think I was trying to get you more students. Now I just want to get rid of the ones you already have."

Wren walked toward her again, then stopped and held her hands up in surrender. "I can't touch you again right now, or I'll never make it through the lesson. Will you have dinner with me tonight? Up at my house. We can, um, talk about the blog."

Gina laughed. "Sure," she said, injecting as much skepticism into her voice as she could. "We'll discuss your blog."

Wren grinned at her. "Or not."

Wren sighed again and opened the door just as a woman and small boy came into view outside of the office window.

"Can I bring anything?" Gina asked as Wren was walking out. "Flint and steel for the cooking fire?"

"Not in my house," Wren said, giving her a mock offended look. "But on your way over, look for a couple of sticks we can rub together."

Gina laughed and sat down at the desk again, resting her forehead on her closed laptop. Their meeting had taken a dangerous turn in the middle when she had steered the conversation back to Wren's childhood, but it had ended well.

She sat up again and put the back of her hand against her warm cheek. Yes, she really liked the way it had ended.

CHAPTER THIRTEEN

W ren would have liked some time to pull herself together before talking to anyone, but she met up with Linda and Eric right outside the office door. She breathed a quick sigh of relief that she had at least heard them drive in. The office had large picture windows facing into the barn, offering little in the way of privacy. She wasn't happy about being interrupted, but she was grateful to have gotten away without her and Gina being caught.

Eric stopped making engine noises long enough to shout a greeting to her as he raced past and into the tack room to get Callie's saddle.

"Is he being a rocket ship again?" she asked Linda, who was trailing behind at a much slower pace.

Linda shook her head. "Race car. It's an entirely different sound." She frowned. "Are you all right? You look flushed. Are you getting the flu that's going around?"

Wren put a hand to her chest. "I'm fine," she said, glancing toward the office before she could stop herself. The door was closed, but she could see Gina through the glass, sitting at the desk watching them, probably waiting for them to move away from the door so she could make her escape. "It's really hot today."

"It's in the low fifties," Linda said as she followed Wren's glance, looking over her shoulder and into the office. She waved at Gina, who sketched a quick wave in return, then started shuffling through her stack of papers, giving a poor impression of someone who was actually reading them. Linda turned back to Wren and gave her a nudge in the shoulder. "I think what you meant to say is *she's* really hot today."

She laughed and went over to help her son, who had emerged from the tack room with his small arms full of equipment, trailing reins and a saddle blanket behind him.

Damn. Wren had been a little too quick to congratulate herself on having a stealth make-out session in the office. She looked at Gina again, who mouthed the word *Sorry* at her. Wren grinned and shook her head, walking backward toward the crossties for a few steps before turning away from Gina and continuing down the aisle. She wasn't sorry at all.

She was glad this lesson was with Eric—if she had to stop kissing Gina and teach anyone at all—even though he came as a package deal with an overly perceptive mother. She didn't think he listened to more than ten percent of her instructions, anyway, so she was free to let her mind wander, calling out an occasional reminder to put his heels down and mainly making sure he was safe on Callie. Linda, Dianna, or any of her other more mature riders would have noticed her uncharacteristic lack of concentration. Eric, on the other hand, was thrilled because she let him trot more than usual.

She was amazed she was able to teach at all, let alone walk and talk in a reasonably normal manner. Gina had caught her by surprise today. The kiss, as delicious as it had been, hadn't felt like an isolated event, but like it was part of the more encompassing experience of being with Gina. Talking to her, sharing untouched parts of her childhood with her, kissing her…everything felt connected somehow. Wren had friends who understood, people whose company she enjoyed. She'd had lovers who had excited her. She had never met someone who seemed to have the potential to be *everything* to her. And someone who made her want to return the favor a thousandfold.

Wren stumbled over the arena's short rail. She had been walking beside Eric and Callie and had continued on instead of turning the corner with them. She sternly pulled more of her focus back to the lesson, drilling Eric on the parts of the horse. He protested until she changed the game and pretended Callie was a dragon he was riding, and then he got most of the answers correct. She filed the idea away for future lessons, even though she thought Callie looked about as undragonlike as it was possible for a horse to look. If it got him to pay attention and learn something, she'd play along.

Wren managed to keep her mind mostly on the lesson and off her confusing thoughts about Gina until they brought Callie back to the barn and she was free to mentally wander again. Her mind drifted back in time, replaying her conversation with Gina about her resistance to using computers. It was a potent feeling, to be understood like that. Even though Gina's theories weren't one hundred percent accurate, they were insightful and thought-provoking. And they proved she had been thinking about Wren, wondering about her and trying to figure her out.

How perfect it would be if the only reason Wren avoided technology was because she had weird jealousy issues about her parents' little bundle of computer code. Gina's theories had merit, and they were probably tangled up in Wren's decisions, but she had made an affirmative choice to live the way she did. She chose this lifestyle because it emphasized and protected the things she valued. She might try using the computer as a business tool, but like the office phone, it wouldn't infringe on her home. Gina wasn't as ruled by her tech as Wren had initially expected. She didn't take calls or zone out with her phone in the middle of conversations. When she was talking to Wren, she always felt fully present.

But no matter how apparently easy it was for Gina to be away from her computer or phone for lengths of time, she'd never want to live full-time without them. Wren needed to remember that when she started thinking of phrases like *Gina could be everything*. Because, in truth, she couldn't. And Wren wouldn't sacrifice her own values and completely lose sight of who she was, no matter how wonderful the kisses or conversation, and she'd never want Gina to give those things up for her, either. She wasn't about to let herself forget what Gina had said about feeling isolated on the farm, as if she was on the outskirts of not just the physical city, but the career opportunities it represented. Wren didn't know enough about Gina's business to know if she was correct about this location being a huge disadvantage for her, and she hoped Gina might be able to find a way to remain connected to her world without needing to actually live within the city limits.

Wren checked Eric's bridle to make sure it had been cleaned properly, and then she did her evening chores before heading back to her house. She hadn't seen even a glimpse of Gina after Linda and Eric had arrived, and she wondered if Gina was wrestling with the shift in their relationship, too. Wren was kind of glad they had this time apart before their dinner together. She, at least, had needed to work through the excitement of the kiss and get back to a sensible, practical frame of mind. Gina had never hidden who she was or where and how she wanted to spend her life, and neither had Wren, and that was fine. They could move forward—and after a kiss like that, Wren didn't want to move back and pretend it hadn't happened. She wanted forward, even though it had limits. She had analyzed and accepted them. She'd be fine.

That is, as long as she could ignore the part of her mind that was laughing hysterically at her overly cocky assertions.

Wren fed Biscuit, then took a shower and put on a pair of faded jeans and a black T-shirt. Her version of formal wear. She was pulling some ingredients for dinner out of the fridge when the doorbell rang, and Biscuit went berserk.

She answered the door with what she knew was a borderline goofy grin, but she didn't care because Gina looked happy to see her, too. She had changed into a navy-blue crepe shirt with a delicate pattern embroidered around its Henley-style neckline. Wren wanted to trace those soft-looking patterns with her fingers. Her hands were mentally wandering even lower when she felt Grover lick her hand in greeting. She reached down to pet him and then momentarily forgot about Gina's shirt. Well, almost.

"What have you done to my dog?" she asked, walking around him while he calmly stood in place.

"What do you mean?" Gina asked, shutting the door and leaning back against it.

"What do I *mean*?" Wren wasn't sure where to start. She remembered the green paint from this morning, but now there was bright yellow added to the mix. Not to mention the strip of brown running along one side, from his chest into his tail. It was stiff but still a little tacky to the touch. Some kind of wood stain. "What happened to the hair on his neck?"

Gina had one hand over her mouth, and if she was trying to hide her laughter from Wren, it wasn't working. "He likes to be underfoot," she said, not really answering the question. "And he's so quiet I sometimes forget he's there."

"So you paint him like a piece of furniture?"

"Accidentally. If I was painting him on purpose, I'd do something less abstract. Polka dots might be nice."

"Did you accidentally cut his hair?"

Gina came closer and ruffled the uneven clumps on the back of Grover's neck. "A little glue dripped on him. I couldn't wash it out, so I thought I'd just cut off the sticky bits. He has so much hair, who knew it would be this obvious if he was missing some of it?"

"Yeah, who could possibly have known?" Wren laughed. With Gina standing this close, she was ready to forget all about paint drips and bald patches. She might even agree to the polka dots.

Grover trotted into the kitchen, and Wren heard him lapping from the water bowl. He seemed unfazed by his new multicolored appearance. "Anything else I should know about?"

"Well, I'm certainly not telling you about the stuff I managed to clean off him," Gina said, walking past her and starting a circuit of the room. "You have a lot of things."

"I have a fairly normal amount of things." Gina had sounded surprised, so Wren looked around, trying to see the room from another person's perspective. Stacks of books covered most surfaces, the majority of them related to horses and training, but with some thrillers and a range of nonfiction topics thrown in. A couch, two chairs, a coffee table. Add a television, and she thought it would be a pretty standard living room. Well, except for the pile of horse-related tack and other paraphernalia covering the dining room table. She really should have moved it before her company had arrived.

Gina picked up a book about the early Scandinavian settlers in Poulsbo and set it down again after skimming the back cover. "I guess I thought you were more of a minimalist. I expected maybe a futon and a single chair, not this."

"You've seen my barn and office. I don't think either of those could have given you the impression that I'm a minimalist." She walked past Gina and gave her a quick kiss on the cheek on her way to the kitchen. "Is ravioli okay for dinner?"

"Sounds good," Gina said. She stayed in the living room instead of following immediately after Wren, trying to reconcile this house with the picture she'd had in her mind. To be honest, she had been imagining something more along the lines of *Little House on the Prairie*, complete with old-fashioned quilts and solid, plain wooden furniture. Dirt floors, maybe. Burlap sacks for curtains. This room had nothing in common with her vision. The gray maple hardwood flooring was elegant, with unusual patterns of knots and whorls, and Gina thought it might be reclaimed barn wood. She had seen articles about the hot trend, but she would bet that Wren had opted for it because it made environmental sense, and obviously not because it was the latest fad. She probably had no idea how cool she was.

Wren seemed to favor furniture with interesting details, and her pieces looked handmade with fancy scrollwork or delicately turned legs. A matte black woodstove was the one nod to prairie life in the room, but it was more modern with its clean and simple lines than rustic in style. The walls were covered with framed pictures—all of them photographs, both portraits of horses and nature photos of local mountains and fields full of wildflowers.

This was a home. A place to relax and read at night, or a place to invite friends for meals and laughter. A place to snuggle together on the couch and talk about all sorts of inconsequential things that meant the world because they were shared. Gina had tried to turn Wren's house, her world, into the most inhospitable environment she could imagine. The reality of it was frightening because it was familiar. She wasn't supposed to be able to picture herself here, in this off-the-grid, backwater place.

Gina paused by a picture of a teenage Wren standing next to a small bay with Appaloosa markings, her arm draped companionably over the horse's neck as she smiled happily at the camera. Gina thought this looked like the same horse the little boy had been riding today. She had watched a few minutes of the lesson, standing deep in the shadows of the barn, torn between relief at the chance to get a little distance from Wren and wanting to drag her up to the apartment and kiss her where they couldn't be interrupted.

Gina stepped away from the picture and went into the kitchen. Putting an afternoon of distance between herself and Wren hadn't done anything to change her feelings. Gina wanted her with a ferocity that was as unfamiliar as it was frightening. In her past relationships, Gina had always hoped increased intimacy would begin to wear away the edges of her awkwardness, until she was able to totally relax and be herself, but she had always been disappointed. Even months of conversations and flirtations with other women had never brought her to the same level of comfort she had felt with Wren from the first moment they met in the parking lot, with no need to chase after it between the sheets.

Wren's kitchen was all warm oak and buttery yellows and golds. She was standing at a butcher-block counter, cracking an egg into the crater of a small flour mountain and then mixing it together with her graceful fingers.

"You're making ravioli," Gina said, coming to stand next to her and focusing on the food, not her memories of those same fingers lost in her hair and skimming her throat.

"I am," Wren said, bumping Gina with her shoulder while she kept mixing and kneading the dough. "Just like I said I was going to."

Gina shifted behind her and propped her chin on Wren's

shoulder, watching her steadily work the dough together. "No, I mean you're *making* it. From scratch. As opposed to opening a packet and throwing it in boiling water."

Wren laughed, and Gina felt the vibrations move through her where her body was in contact with Wren's. She liked the feeling, so she moved closer, sliding her hands around Wren's stomach. Wren sighed against her, her hands going still as Gina kissed her neck. She rested her mouth softly against Wren's skin, feeling the thrum of her heartbeat against her lips, licking the hollow above her collarbone where the friction of her rougher tongue against Wren's soft skin made Gina ache with wanting her.

Wren twisted her head around until her mouth met Gina's, kissing her slowly and deeply while she turned the rest of her body to face her. Gina felt each inch of movement as Wren's arm rubbed across her chest, soon replaced by the pressure of Wren's breasts and hips against her own.

Gina pulled back from the kiss just a fraction, remaining close enough so she felt Wren's quick exhales against her mouth. "You'd better not put those hands in my hair until after you wash them," she said, emphasizing her threat with a gentle rasp of her teeth against Wren's lower lip.

Wren moaned at the bite, then rested her forehead against Gina's and laughed quietly. "Don't worry. If I get dough in your hair, we can just cut it out. It's thick enough no one will notice if some is missing."

Gina pushed away from Wren with a grin and leaned her elbow on the counter, not going far from her. "I'm not showing up in my videos with a haircut like Grover's. Now keep cooking," she said motioning toward the lump of dough on the counter. "It's very sexy."

"This is sexy?"

Wren wriggled her dough-covered fingers at Gina, and she laughed and swatted them away. "How'd you learn to cook like this?"

"Neither of my parents likes to cook, and they were usually too wrapped up in their latest project to spend time in the kitchen, anyway. We had a lot of takeout and frozen meals, but when I stopped eating meat, I had a hard time making that style of eating work for me. I got some cookbooks from the library and started experimenting. My parents ate whatever I put on the table. I don't think they even realized that they became vegetarians."

Gina watched Wren flatten the dough by passing it back and forth through a pasta machine, before pushing it into a metal mold and filling it with a mixture of ricotta, parmesan, and spinach. They kept the conversation light, talking about favorite meals and childhood hobbies, but Gina felt something more profound hovering in the space between them. Something intimate and domestic and tempting. Her physical response to Wren was much easier to handle, and Gina crossed the distance between them often, with soft touches, kisses, and playful shoves.

Wren's house seemed full to her now, with its books and photos, its inviting kitchen and the rich scents of Wren's thoughtfully crafted meal. And Wren, laughing and chatting as she created magic with her hands. But Gina knew this wouldn't last. It was exciting because it was new for her. Too many nights like this, with no sounds of television or YouTube videos in the background, no busy city streets just outside the door, and Gina would grow as resentful as she had been as a teenager.

She reached for Wren and kissed her, pushing her hard against the counter and driving away the knowledge that she really wasn't missing any of those things at all.

Chapter Fourteen

S he won't want to do this," Gina said, walking down the stairs of her apartment the next morning. She kept one hand on the rail to steady herself and keep from tripping over Grover since she was trying to walk and talk to Maia at the same time.

"I don't care how much she hates phones. She can't date my best friend without getting my approval first. So unless she wants to fly to Nashville, she'd better talk to me this way."

"We're not dating," Gina protested, although there had certainly been enough kissing last night to qualify. She had been tempted to stay the night, and she could tell Wren had wanted her to, as well, given how reluctant she had been to let Gina go after she had walked her back to the apartment. Something had held Gina back, though, and she had finally pulled out of the circle of Wren's arms and gone inside. Her resistance wasn't strong enough to last—she was surprised she had made it this long, in fact—but she was desperately trying to hang on to her determination to maintain emotional distance. Each line would get easier to cross, and moving forward from laughing together to touching to kissing had felt so natural. If she went too far beyond kissing, she might never make it back to where she belonged. She was already dealing with the stress of commuting to Seattle for photo trips and business meetings. She refused to believe she had lost any of her passion for her work, but she sometimes ended up staying on the farm instead of going to the city for inconsequential reasons. If she had a reason as all-encompassing as being in bed with Wren, she'd probably never get back on that damned ferry.

"Yeah, sure, you're not dating," Maia said in a disbelieving tone. "You're just spending time together, making out, feeding each other…"

"As friends. And we don't feed each other." Okay, at one point during the evening, she might have licked some caramel sauce off Wren's fingers, but that wasn't really romantic—she had merely been taste-testing dessert. And she hadn't mentioned anything about it to Maia, so she was prepared to deny it to the end.

"Then you do admit to making out with her," Maia said with a grin.

Damn. Gina hadn't mentioned any of the kissing to her, either. "I admit to nothing," she said. She hesitated at the edge of the barn and peered into the arena. "And she's riding right now, so maybe the two of you can talk later."

"Let me see."

Gina sighed and turned her phone around. She felt too much like a stalker hiding in the shadows and pointing a phone at Wren, so she walked into the open and headed to the arena.

"Walk steadier, or I'm going to be sick…Wow, she really is beautiful."

"I know, right?" Gina paused on the hill while Biscuit and Grover milled around her legs. Wren continued to ride, completely focused on her horse in a way Gina loved to witness. Her intensity and passion were such an interesting contrast to her more playful side, and Gina loved them both. *Liked* them, she corrected herself.

Gina turned the phone around again so she and Maia could see each other. "Too bad she's working right now, or you could have talked to her. Well, I should go—"

"Edit me out," Wren called.

"I'm not filming," Gina yelled back. "If I was, I'd make sure I was facing away from you."

"Oh my God, you two are so cute. Take me over there."

Gina sighed and walked over to where Wren and Foam were standing near the entrance to the arena.

She hoped Wren would flat-out refuse to talk, although she felt silly for feeling that way. She wasn't sure why she was so reluctant for them to meet. She had met plenty of Wren's friends, but somehow this was different since Gina's social circle was so much smaller than Wren's seemed to be. Introducing her to Maia was, for Gina, the equivalent of bringing a girlfriend home to meet her family. "Maia wants to meet you," she said.

"Seriously? You named your phone Maia? I know you love your technology, Gina, but this might be taking it too far. What's next, are you going to start buying it clothes?" Wren gave an exaggerated gasp. "That's why you wanted that little antique dresser. Not for herbs, but for all your teeny phone clothes."

"She's funny. Hand me over."

Wren swung out of her saddle and gestured for Gina's phone. "Yes, hand her over. Is it your friend from Tennessee?"

"Um, yes," Gina said, surprised by Wren's enthusiastic response. She pointed at the lens on her phone. "This is the camera. Aim it at yourself so she can see you."

"Okay. Oh, hey! You're so clear, it's like you're right here, not halfway across the country."

"I hope it's not too frightening for you," Maia said, and Gina could hear the laughter in her voice. "Gina told me you're a bit of a technophobe, so maybe we should have eased you into this by taping a photo of me on the phone first."

Wren winced. "One of those newfangled photographs? I don't know, maybe we should start with a daguerreotype and work up from there."

Wren unbuckled her helmet and handed it and Foam's reins to Gina. "He still needs to cool down. Do you mind hopping up and walking him around for a while? I'll give Maia a tour of the farm."

She walked off, chatting on the cell as if she hadn't been bemoaning the loss of her tin cans only weeks earlier. Gina watched her go, feeling as if she'd been dropped into some sort of alternate universe, where Wren was happily embracing technology, and she was standing in the middle of an arena holding a horse.

Foam nudged her gently with his muzzle, and Gina shrugged and twisted her hair into a makeshift ponytail, tucking it under the helmet and buckling the strap under her chin. She had gotten accustomed to being around Wren's horses, even though they had initially been triggers to remind her of junior high. Although they were no longer stress-inducing, she still hadn't felt an urge to ride any of them, but she couldn't be a coward now and simply lead Foam around the arena. Not when Wren was bravely letting a cell phone get close enough to her to manipulate her brain waves, or whatever she was afraid it might do.

She used the mounting block to help her get on since Foam was a lot taller than the small quarter horses she had ridden in school. Wider, too, she discovered once she was in the saddle. Foam started walking hesitatingly around the ring, but once she stopped worrying about his every step and relaxed, he did, too. After a few circuits of the arena, she decided she kind of liked the view from horseback, especially since her main focus was on Wren, who was walking near the paddocks with her dogs right at her heels, laughing and talking with Maia. Gina waited for a sting of jealousy, since Wren had a natural way of connecting with everyone she met, and Gina had never been able to think of herself as having the same gift, but all she felt was grateful to Wren for stepping into her world for at least this moment.

Gina knew Wren was making an effort to get to know Maia because of how important she was in Gina's life. Envy might have been preferable to the heat that stirred inside her when Wren looked over and smiled at her—if Wren's agreeable attitude toward the phone call had left Gina with any doubts about Wren's feelings for her, the expression on her face just now squashed them completely. She smiled in return as Wren came back down the hill, turning the phone so Maia could see her.

"Look, it's Gina on a horse. For the first time since coming here."

Gina dismounted and handed the reins back to Wren, taking her phone in return. She wasn't about to make a permanent swap, but it had been fun to trade places for a little while.

"How was the tour?" she asked Maia, standing close enough to Wren for them both to be visible on the screen.

"Great! It's such a beautiful farm. You know, she could probably make a fortune renting out your apartment as an Airbnb."

"A what?" Wren asked, elbowing Gina in the side.

Gina moved out of Wren's range and headed toward the barn. "I hadn't thought of that, but you're right. People would love to stay here instead of a hotel. With these water views and all this peace and quiet..."

"But still close to Seattle..." Maia continued.

"And hiking and boating. Oh, she could build a boat dock down by the water and rent out kayaks."

"*She's* pretty sure the zoning permits would be astronomical," Wren said, grabbing the back of Gina's shirt to slow her down.

Gina tried to pull away, laughing at the thought of Wren having to face a new set of visitors every weekend. "The horses would be a big draw," she said to Maia. "She could do pony rides if the guests have little kids."

"*She's* selling all the horses and replacing them with very mean snakes," Wren said, wrapping her arm around Gina's waist when she stopped struggling to get away.

"I'm going to go film now and let the two of you sort this out," Maia said with a smile. "Thanks again for showing me around, Wren. Promise I can come stay, even if you don't open to the general public?"

"Of course. But just you, and only for one night. Maybe only an hour or two if I'm in a bad mood."

Maia grinned. "A whole weekend, and I'm bringing my husband. Plus, we'll want one of those pony rides."

She ended the call before Wren could stop laughing and respond. Gina put her phone in the pocket of her jeans and stepped away from Wren's touch as they went into the barn. She propped her elbows on the open door of an empty stall and watched Wren untack her horse.

"Joking aside, it's a really good idea," Gina said. She held up a hand to stop Wren's protest. "I don't expect you to turn this place into a guest ranch, but what if you meet some people online who want to ride with you even though they don't live close? I can see someone coming here from another state, or even country, for a week's worth of lessons. Not all the time, but maybe once in a while."

"Or someone who can come teach a clinic for me and my

students." Wren clapped a hand over her mouth, then lowered it slowly. "Now you've got me doing it," she said, shaking her head as she continued unbuckling Foam's girth.

Gina smiled. Wren seemed to have a natural tendency to want to learn and grow, but she had somehow gotten into the habit of stifling it and hiding behind her equally strong bent toward maintaining the status quo, afraid to let anyone or anything new come into her life in case it devalued what she already had. Gina felt as if she was helping Wren explore possibilities she hadn't considered before—ones that would add value to her world, not take it away—just like Wren had helped her by getting her out from behind her screens.

Gina had used the internet to make friends when she couldn't in person and had eventually stopped trying to find any connections in her real life, but these days she was spending more and more time unplugged—more and more time seeking Wren's company. She halted her train of thought. Yes, they were good for each other, but was any of this good for Gina's career? Since moving here, she was already finding it too easy to make excuses, to avoid pushing herself into the social situations that would advance her career. She and Wren could continue to grow individually once Gina moved back to the city and Wren moved on with her own life.

"Well, it's something to think about," Gina said. "Don't stop yourself from coming up with options since you only need to follow through with them if you want to. The more ideas you have, the more likely you'll be to find the ones that really fit."

"I'll think about it," Wren agreed. She handed Gina a brush and then picked up her saddle and bridle. "For now, though, the apartment is yours."

"For now," Gina said with a slight shrug, walking over to Foam and starting to groom him without meeting Wren's eyes.

Wren went into the tack room and put her saddle and bridle near the sink. She picked up a damp sponge and rubbed it over a bar of saddle soap, needing a few moments to herself. Gina had mentioned finding what really fit, and all Wren could think of was how Gina herself seemed to be the perfect fit in her life. Wren loved how Gina challenged her to be more open to new ideas, and at the same time how comfortable it was to be with her. She just wasn't sure where she stood with Gina.

She was confident that Gina felt the same about her on a physical level, especially after the evening before. Gina also seemed to enjoy spending time with her, since she could easily have shut herself in the apartment with her computer—as Wren had initially expected her to do—instead of seeking her out.

Gina's repetition of the phrase *for now* was another one of those moments when Wren felt doubt creep in and take hold. Gina had never lied and had always been honest about wanting this to be a temporary stop in her life, but Wren wished she wouldn't keep pulling back. That she would be as wholeheartedly in their relationship while they were together as Wren was trying to be.

She scrubbed the bridle's noseband, removing all traces of sweat and dirt as she reconsidered her wish. Maybe Gina was playing this the right way, keeping some balance between having fun together in the present and acknowledging the truth about their future. Wren probably should follow her example, or she was going to be the one who ended up hurt.

She hung the bridle back on its hook and returned to the barn aisle, where she saw Gina standing next to Foam's head, scratching his favorite spot behind his ears. She had to stretch to reach, and her T-shirt had pulled up enough to show the curve of her waist. Oh, Wren was going to end up hurt, all right. She might as well accept it now and deal with the pain later.

She picked up Foam's fly sheet from where she had left it folded on a tack trunk. "I had a brilliant new idea while I was in there cleaning tack," she said as she put the sheet on her horse. "I think I'll open up my living room to the public and turn my house into a restaurant."

Gina nodded, as if giving the notion serious thought. "I like it. You'll be able to retire on tips alone, with your amazing people skills and sunny disposition."

"Exactly. Although I'd gladly do it for free, just for the chance to have a hundred random strangers invade my home every night."

Gina laughed and handed her Foam's lead rope. "Forget renting out the apartment. You can just have them bring sleeping bags and camp out on your bedroom floor, like a big happy slumber party."

"And then pony rides for everyone in the morning, right, Foam?" Wren smiled when Gina caught her hand as they walked toward the paddocks. "I probably should get to work on perfecting my recipes, then, in anticipation of the big crowds. I need to learn how to defrost frozen meals, and I probably should invest in a microwave if I want to serve real quality food."

"Tourists will flock here in droves," Gina said, giving Wren's hand a squeeze before letting go.

Wren stayed close beside her. "Since this is all your fault...I mean, your brilliant idea, how about going on a practice pony ride? I can take you to a spot with the best view of the Olympics. Just think what a great photo op that'll be."

Gina paused midstride. She felt some misgivings about spending too much time on a horse, but her social media brain was already planning how to turn a single ride into several posts. "Um, sure," she said.

Even though her response to the invitation was lukewarm,

Wren's answering smile was anything but. "Wonderful," she said. "I'll grab a couple horses for us while you change into something you don't mind getting dirty."

Yay. Dirt. Gina headed toward her apartment, trying to convince herself that she was doing this for the sake of some interesting photos, not because she would grab on to any excuse to spend time with Wren.

CHAPTER FIFTEEN

Gina went upstairs and changed into an older pair of jeans and a long-sleeved dark purple shirt. She had enjoyed a brief moment in Wren's world when it merely consisted of a few laps of the arena on Foam, but she wasn't sure how she felt about an hour or so in the saddle. Horseback riding had been bundled with most of her other childhood activities and filed in the never-doing-that-again category in her mind. Riding with Wren seemed miles away from her past experiences, though, and Gina was willing to give it a try. She was already planning the captions for her photos, and she hadn't even gotten on the horse yet. Her social media career had been good for her in that regard—she tried to be more open about new experiences because she wanted to document them online.

She jogged down the stairs, hoping Wren would find her a quieter, smaller horse to ride. Maybe the little Appaloosa mare that Eric had ridden? Foam had been well-behaved in the arena, but he had felt a little too powerful beneath her. Plus, she didn't think it would take him long to figure out that he knew far more than she did about riding and possibly decide it wasn't worth the effort of carrying her around. She wanted some photos from the higher vantage point a horse would afford her, not some from ground level, watching her mount race back toward the barn without her.

She walked into the barn and saw two horses waiting in the crossties while Wren got their tack ready. Wren grinned when she saw Gina and tugged playfully on the sleeve of her shirt.

"You look beautiful. Purple really does suit you."

Gina laughed. "Would it horrify you to know I only chose this shirt because the front pocket has a button? I was worried about my cell phone falling out."

Wren shook her head. "It makes perfect sense to me. I only picked these pants because they have a pocket, and I was worried about losing my high-tech gaming console." She fished a piece of paper out of her pocket and unfolded it to reveal a partially finished crossword puzzle.

"You have one puzzle. I have access to millions of them," Gina said, wiggling her phone at Wren before buttoning it safely away. "I'm assuming that one's mine," Gina added, pointing at the shorter of the two horses. He had a nondescript look about him, as if he'd blend into the background at any barn with at least one other dark brown horse in it. He was standing with his coarse-looking head lowered and his eyes halfway closed, looking supremely bored by the prospect of a ride. His neighbor, on the other hand, was watching Wren's every move with pricked ears. He was taller than Foam, with a delicate, well-bred look about him that even Gina could recognize as a sign of quality.

Wren laughed and handed her a brush, aiming her toward the tall chestnut instead of her preferred bay. "Nope. Unless you want to trade, of course. The first time I took the Duke on a trail ride he threw me into the bay. Literally into the water. On purpose, I'm sure. You get to ride Kingfisher. He's a rescued ex-racehorse and is about as quiet as can be."

Gina wanted to feel reassured by Wren's words, but her mind snagged on the word *racehorse*. She hoped he was more inclined to amble than race now that his career was over. She stood on her toes in an effort to reach the top of her horse's neck with the brush. "I've forgotten how to measure a horse's height. What is he, about one hundred hands?"

"Close," Wren said, sharing an exaggerated eye roll with Kingfisher as she walked past him to get her saddle. "He's seventeen three. He'll take good care of you, but the offer to trade is still on the table if you don't trust me."

Gina pretended to consider the swap, even though she trusted Wren's judgment without question. "Did he really buck you off?" she asked, gesturing toward Wren's horse, skeptical not only because the animal in question looked incapable of moving faster than a walk, but mainly because she had seen Wren ride. "I've seen you out there on Foam, and I'd be surprised if any horse outside of a rodeo bronc could get you out of the saddle. Even in a rodeo, I'd bet on you."

Wren looked pleased. "Thank you. That's a nice compliment." She shrugged and gave Gina one of her wry grins. "Unfortunately, I was feeling the same confidence in my superior riding skills, and he decided it was his duty to prove just how wrong I was. He came here for training because his owner is terrified of him, and we had a few major battles when he first arrived. He had been well-behaved for about a week when I decided to take him on a nice little walk along the beach. I was meandering along, congratulating myself on what an amazing trainer I was, and the next thing I knew, I was sitting on my ass in the bay before I even realized he was about to buck."

She chuckled and gave the dozing horse a pat on the neck, as if acknowledging him as a worthy opponent. Gina smiled in return, admiring the ease with which Wren could laugh at herself. There was a sense of spontaneity in the way she talked, without needing to filter her words or worry about the impression she might be making. It felt very different from

Gina's usual interactions with people. She could tell humorous stories about herself, and she never tried to give the impression that she was perfect, but she always felt the underlying need to present a polished self both online and in person. Even her chattier videos, where she answered viewer questions and talked without a script, were edited with the audience's reactions in mind—whether they were followers or sponsors. Gina had never felt as if she had the gift of just being herself, unless she was speaking from the other side of a lens or screen. She sometimes felt close to it with Maia, but never as much as she did when she was with Wren.

"I suppose he hasn't been able to get you off since, right?" Gina asked, buckling Kingfisher's girth loosely around his belly.

"Oh, I really wish I could say you're right, but I can't." Wren came over and handed her a pair of black leather ankle-high boots. "You should wear these instead of your tennis shoes. They're safer for riding."

Gina perched on a wooden step stool and exchanged her sneakers for the sturdier boots. "There's another advantage of being online," Gina said. "You can edit out the falls."

"If I could edit out the bruises, both to my ego and my ass, then you might just convince me," Wren said, double-checking both horses' bridles before handing Gina a riding helmet and leading the way out of the barn.

Even with the help of the mounting block, Gina's attempt to climb into the saddle was far from graceful. "I should have brought gum to chew," she said as they started walking along the path toward the water. "I need something to keep my ears from popping at this altitude."

She felt a little nervous for the first few minutes, but once she got accustomed to having the ground so far away, she started to relax. Wren's quiet voice helped, too, as she gave

Gina some basic pointers on riding English instead of the Western style she had originally learned. Kingfisher lived up to Wren's promises, not even tensing up when Duke wheeled with startling swiftness and tried to run back to the barn. Wren calmly got him back in line, and Gina took one hand off the reins long enough to unbutton her shirt pocket and take out her phone.

"Are you hoping to get a picture of me falling off?" Wren asked.

"Of course not," Gina said with a reassuring shake of her head. "I'm switching to video mode. A simple picture wouldn't do it justice."

"Oh, very nice," Wren said. "Maybe we can switch horses on the way back, and I'll do the filming."

Gina gripped both reins and a hunk of Kingfisher's mane in her left hand and took a picture with her right of a hawk perched on a nearby branch, calmly watching them walk past. "Sure," she said, moving the camera around to get a shot of Wren with nothing but gray-blue bay as a backdrop. "If you can show me how to activate the camera, I'll let you hold the phone."

"Damn," Wren said, guiding Duke around a fallen tree. "I guess I'm destined to be the entertainment, and you're destined to document it."

They fell silent, and the only sounds were birdsong, the water gently lapping against the rocky shore, and the crunching sound of the horses' hooves as they walked through the loose pebbles. Gina took dozens of photos, alternating between capturing shots of the beautiful scenery around her and of Wren. Wren was quickly becoming her favorite subject, with her quicksilver changes in expression and athletic way of moving. Since the horses made it impractical for Gina to actually touch her, she did the next best thing by taking photos.

The phone held between them gave her the chance to focus on Wren without her noticing.

"You need to edit me out of those," Wren said. She kept her gaze forward as they left the beach and turned onto a narrow dirt trail, but Gina could see the curve of her smile. Maybe she was noticing more than Gina realized.

"No way. I'm building a website for your farm, and I need lots of pictures." She saw Wren about to protest and continued. "Yes, you need to be in them. Potential clients need to see how well you ride. And how gracefully you fall."

"Well, unless you want your phone to fall, you might want to tuck it back in its pocket." Wren reached across the space between them and patted Gina softly on the chest. "We're going up a fairly steep hill."

Gina fumbled with her reins and phone for a moment, disconcerted by Wren's touch, but managed to get her cell buttoned away and her hold on Kingfisher reorganized before they started up the incline. She and Wren had been playfully physical from the start, with light shoves and shoulder bumps, but now every touch seemed to carry with it echoes from the kisses they had shared. She tried to read Wren's expression to see if she was having similar responses to contact, but she couldn't tell since the path ahead of them narrowed, and Wren moved Duke into the lead.

"Lean forward like I am," Wren called out to her. "And don't hesitate to grab a little mane to keep your balance."

Gina shifted her weight forward. She hadn't let go of Kingfisher's mane since she had climbed on him, and she was sure Wren knew it, but she appreciated the reassurance that she was making the right choice in opting for a feeling of security over the concern about whether she looked foolish or scared.

After the first few yards, Gina started to feel an ache in her thighs from holding herself out of the saddle and balanced over Kingfisher's shoulders. Even walking on flat ground would have been taxing to muscles unaccustomed to riding— or doing much exercise beyond walking city streets, if she was being honest—but the hilly terrain was sapping her strength. The slope steepened sharply, and she was about to just let go and slide backward, landing blissfully on the ground, when her horse came to a halt.

Any complaints she wanted to make about sore muscles vanished from her mind as she gazed at the vista spread before her. A fir-covered valley stretched before her, offering glimpses of some of the Sound's many arms. The jagged line of the Olympics rose over the top of the ridge across from them, closer than Gina had realized since they were mostly hidden from sight on Wren's farm. Another hawk made lazy circles off to her right.

"Do you want to get down and take some pictures?" Wren dismounted and draped Duke's reins over her arm as she came to Gina's side. "Let me help."

Gina swung her leg over Kingfisher's back and slid down his side, glad to have Wren standing nearby since the long drop combined with her aching legs put her off balance. Wren put a steadying hand on her back and then wrapped one arm around Gina's middle and gave her a quick kiss on the neck. She stepped away again, as if the touch and kiss had been casual and natural. There was nothing casual about Gina's response, though.

Wren took Kingfisher's reins from her, and Gina walked forward until she had a clearer view of the Olympics. She took several shots of the mountains and some close-ups of the shrubs around her before turning around and snapping a quick picture of Wren with the two horses.

"Edit me *out*," Wren protested. Gina just grinned, quickly scrolling through the alerts she had received during their ride.

"What's on there, anyway?" Wren asked.

Gina came closer and angled her screen so Wren could see the readout. "This is my Instagram page, and these are comments on my posts that have come in since we left the barn. This number is new followers, and this one shows how many people liked my posts."

Wren gave a low whistle. "Those are huge numbers," she said.

Gina shrugged. "Moderately. My goal is a million."

"And then?"

"Two million, I guess." Gina paused. "Does it seem superficial to you, this obsession with numbers?"

Wren handed her Kingfisher's reins again. "Not at all. First, I know you well enough by now not to ever assign the word *superficial* to anything you care about." She paused and rested her palm on Gina's cheek. The meaning behind her words, as well as her touch, made Gina feel a flush of heat. The intimacy of being known and respected was potent.

"Second," Wren continued, "I'm the same way when I compete. If I scored ten on every movement in a dressage test, I would celebrate for about five minutes, and then I'd be planning to move up a level at the next show and challenge myself even more. The numbers matter, but it's because of what they represent. Hard work, learning…everything that has gone into building them."

Gina leaned forward and kissed Wren, pressing flush against her when Wren slid her free hand into the loose hair at the base of Gina's neck and tugged her forward. She had instinctively sensed the value of her numbers, but she had never articulated it the way Wren just had. She realized what it meant about Wren's feelings for her if she was able to look objectively at tech-based demographics and see the real-life value in them. Somehow, Wren's comments made their relationship feel deeper than any physical intimacy could do.

They broke apart when Duke stomped his hoof impatiently. "You're for sale. Cheap," Wren told him as she reached for Gina's knee to give her a leg up on Kingfisher. Her hand lingered for only a moment on Gina's thigh, but she felt the pressure even more acutely than she had felt sore muscles only seconds before.

"Come to my place for dinner again tonight?" Wren asked. "No intrusive horses invited."

Chapter Sixteen

W ren pulled a quiche out of the oven and set it on a trivet to cool. She heard Gina's knock, followed immediately by Biscuit's high-pitched series of yips, and she reviewed her game plan as she walked to the door. *Keep it light. Don't push for more than Gina can give. Just have fun.*

Really, those sentiments sounded nothing like her. All she could do was try, though. She opened the door and stepped aside as the two dogs leaped at each other, leaning across them to give Gina a quick kiss on the cheek.

"You're right on time," she said. "I just took the—"

She wasn't sure how Gina got her there so fast, but suddenly Wren's back was pressed against the closed door and Gina was kissing her with a passion that matched everything Wren felt inside. A small part of her wanted to pause and ask what this meant, and where they were going with their relationship, but the rest of her knew the truth. This meant Gina wanted her as much as she wanted Gina. Where were they going? To the bedroom. Maybe just the couch, since it was closer. That was all Wren needed to know right now. No analyzing, no wondering.

She slid her fingers into Gina's hair, raking the curls back and kissing her way down Gina's exposed neck. She felt Gina's quick pulse against her tongue, felt Gina's low moan vibrate through her lips. Gina's hands were on her hips, then her waist. Under her shirt and cool against Wren's overheated skin.

Wren gasped when Gina's fingertips teased across her breasts, making her nipples feel tight with the pressure of wanting—*needing*—to be closer, to get rid of even the thin barrier of clothing between them. Her muscles felt weak, but she managed to push herself away from the door and lead Gina toward her bedroom.

Gina pulled back slightly, and Wren stopped.

"You cooked for me," Gina said. "It smells good in here. Should we...do we need to eat first?"

Wren shook her head with a laugh. "It's quiche. It's even better cold."

Gina smiled and wrapped her arms around Wren's neck, leaning forward to kiss her again. "Good," she said when they both pulled away, breathless. "I wouldn't want to offend your culinary sensibilities."

"Not a chance," Wren said. She led Gina the rest of the way to her bedroom, shutting the dogs outside the room.

Gina looked around the room, with its simple bed and dresser, and a nightstand with a small stack of books on it. "See? Here's the minimalist look I expected from you."

"All right, then," Wren said, crossing her arms as if settling in for a long conversation. "Let's pause and discuss decorating styles."

"I can't help it," Gina said with a laugh. "You fascinate me."

"And you excite me," Wren said, moving closer and tracing the line of Gina's temple and cheek with the softest of touches. Gina exhaled softly, and Wren felt the feathery touch of Gina's breath against her cheek, followed by the insistent tug of her hands as they unbuttoned Wren's jeans.

"What about this?" Gina asked as her hand slid under

cotton and teased through the wetness Wren felt between her legs. "Does this excite you, too?"

Wren wanted to answer, but her ability to speak evaporated when Gina's fingers reached deeper inside her. She shivered, pouring the intensity of her feelings into a devouring kiss and throwing out all her resolutions to just have fun and keep things light. Gina responded with as much emotion as Wren was feeling, continuing to explore and stroke until Wren was breathless with desire. Gina pushed against her, moving her toward the bed until Wren tumbled backward onto it. She kicked off her jeans, watching Gina do the same, and then Gina was there with her, straddling her hips and rubbing against sensitive flesh that was no longer under Wren's control. She came with a shuddering gasp, reaching between them to touch Gina, caress her, and bring her to an orgasm that echoed through Wren's body, filling every part of her.

❖

Gina started to drift off to sleep with Wren's head resting on her shoulder and her arm draped over Gina's stomach. Her body felt drained, satisfied and weary after being with Wren, but there was a strange ache of longing deep inside her. Oddly enough, she was feeling a pang of sadness because she wanted exactly what she had at the moment—Wren's warm presence wrapped in her arms.

Maybe she was merely anticipating the time when Wren wouldn't be close enough to touch, when they would be separated by miles and not by the few dozen yards between the apartment and the house. Or maybe she was aware of a battle going on between fulfilling the dreams she had had since she was a teenager and giving in to the contentment of being here with Wren. Even the word *contentment* sounded stagnant in her mind. Stifled, closed. Dull. None of those adjectives applied in any way to Wren, but Gina was afraid of them nonetheless.

She shifted, sliding out from under Wren's weight and sitting up on the edge of the bed.

"Are you okay?" Wren asked, her voice sleepy as she rolled over and rubbed her palm over Gina's thigh.

"I'm fine," Gina said, bending down to kiss Wren on the lips, but pulling away again when she felt arousal stirring low in her belly. "I just need to get back. I have a ton of work to do."

Wren propped herself up on one elbow. "You need to get back," she repeated. She laughed, but it didn't seem as natural and easy as usual to Gina. "Because the one-minute commute will be too much in the morning?"

Gina forced a smile, too. She brushed her fingers through Wren's hair, fighting the urge to tighten them and pull Wren closer. "I have so many comments to read and responses to write that I've gotten in the habit of working strange hours. You get some rest, and I'll put in a few hours on my laptop before I go to bed. I have a PR meeting in the city tomorrow morning, but I'll see you when I get back?"

Wren seemed to struggle internally with something, but after a moment of hesitation, she smiled and reached up to where Gina's hand was still entwined in her hair. She pulled it down and kissed Gina's wrist, then let go of her hand.

"Sure," she said, lying back and pulling the covers across her body. "I'll see you in the morning."

Gina nodded, knowing there was so much more she should be saying but not sure how to start. Or how to end. She got dressed quickly and let herself out the front door, wishing she had at least called Grover to come with her.

She walked partway down the path to the barn before she paused and tilted her head, listening to the sounds around her.

She heard the wind swishing through the tallest branches in the fir trees towering on either side of the lane, but there was a different sound layered underneath. She finally traced it to a clump of what she had initially thought was some sort of ivy, but Wren had called Oregon grape. The same breeze through this cluster of bushes sounded different to Gina, like pieces of paper being crushed and rubbed together.

She sighed softly. On her first night here, Wren had told her she would hear things in a new way after spending time in the country and losing her city habit of tuning out most of the noises around her. Wren had been right, and now Gina was noticing nuances in the world that she hadn't sensed before. She wondered how long she'd have to be back in Seattle before she started shutting them out again. She sighed again, quieter than the breeze, and continued on her way.

❖

Wren walked across the empty arena and stepped over the low railing. A three-quarter moon gave plenty of light for her to see as she made her way across the shoreline, with its smooth, round rocks that slid and rolled under her feet. She stood at the bay's edge and let the softly lapping water soak her worn tennis shoes. The shock of cold she felt when the water finally penetrated through her socks was enough to jolt her fully into wakefulness. She looked up at the night sky, hoping to find the sense of peace that usually overcame her when she was totally alone on her farm, but it was elusive tonight.

A thin wisp of a cloud slid across the moon, moved by stronger winds than Wren felt at ground level. She lowered her gaze until she was staring across the bay at the glow from Seattle's lights. She had lived with this view for years, always knowing the city was there, but never feeling an irresistible pull toward it. To her, it was another tool to be used—a place to shop or find entertainment—and not a lifestyle. She knew Gina felt differently about it, somehow believing it was solely responsible for her success, and Wren had to respect that, no matter how hard it was for her to fully understand. She might not be familiar with all the nuances of social media fame, but she knew Gina. She was charismatic and talented, and any success she had was surely due to her own hard work, creativity, and personality. A few square miles of steel and concrete didn't deserve all the credit for her popularity.

Wren turned her back on the water and the city and saw the moment when the apartment light blinked out. *Now* she felt totally alone. Forget opening a restaurant or turning her place into a hotel, her world felt crowded enough right now that if she wanted some alone time, she had to go outside at three in the morning. And Dianna wanted her to be even busier?

Wren tried to laugh at her stupid joke, but it wasn't much fun playing the grouch without Gina there to tease her. And the humor became even weaker when Wren could no longer deny that the privacy she had always cherished felt dimmer now, when all she wanted was to have Gina by her side.

She sighed and squelched her way back to the arena, where pieces of tanbark adhered to her sodden shoes. She paused at the edge and kicked off as much as she could before continuing on her way home. The night with Gina had been amazing, and Wren wanted more—not just more sex, but more of Gina. She wanted as many nights like this as she could get. The price was high, but she wouldn't hesitate to pay it if it meant Gina was even a small part of her life.

She gave a low whistle, and the dogs emerged from the shadows as gray ghosts in the moonlight. They joined her as she walked back to her house and her empty bed.

CHAPTER SEVENTEEN

G ina dragged herself awake, flinching at the sound of the alarm's insistent ring when she wasn't ready to get up. She automatically reached across the bed for Wren, as she had done every morning over the past week, and found nothing to hold on to. Cool sheets, flat and bare. She struggled to a sitting position and finally registered the fact that it was her phone ringing, not an alarm. She hadn't had any need for alarms here on the farm because her sheer curtains let in more than enough light to wake her early every morning.

She didn't recognize the number on the phone, and she answered with her thumb hovering over the *end call* icon, ready to disconnect if someone was trying to sell her something at six in the morning.

"Hello?" She cleared her throat when her voice came out rough with sleep.

"Ms. Strickland? This is Detective Brent from Seattle PD."

"Oh," she breathed softly, her weary mind racing through several dire possible explanations for the call in microseconds. Her parents had been in an accident. Somehow the police knew she tended to drive at least ten miles an hour over the speed limit, and they were calling to fine her for fifteen years of speeding.

Wren. Gina shook her head. Not Wren. They had slept mere yards from each other. If anything had happened to Wren, Gina would know. Wouldn't she? She listened beyond the phone and heard horses neighing and banging their stall doors in the barn below her. She sighed in relief. Wren was feeding her impatient animals. She was okay.

"Ms. Strickland? Are you still there?"

"Yes, I'm sorry. How can I help you?"

"I'm calling about the cyberstalking case you reported last month. The perpetrator posted similar attacks on three other people, and our Computer Crimes Unit was able to identify him. If you can come down to the station, we can discuss how you want to proceed with pressing charges."

Gina gripped her phone, worried it would slip out of her suddenly sweaty palm. Questions tumbled through her head, but only one mattered. "I can go back to my life?" she asked. "Is it really safe to go back?"

"Have you changed the details he made public?"

"Yes. Social Security number, my bank accounts, my address." She had changed her address to a post office box, but she lived at Wren's. She didn't have a place of her own, not really, but now she was being told she had another chance at the city apartment that had always been her goal in life. "I've changed all my passwords, too, and the way I let people comment on my pages."

"You should be okay to go back to normal, but remember that catching one criminal doesn't eradicate the crime. Someone like you, with a high-profile presence online, should be very careful with their private information. We can give you some tips for protecting yourself when you come to the station."

"Yes, thank you. I'll be there in about an hour."

Gina disconnected, then walked to the window with her

arms wrapped around her middle. She should be celebrating. This was what she wanted, what she had assumed would eventually happen. She would be safe to go home, to Seattle. To start her life again, turning back to the moment when it had been so horribly disrupted, and moving forward again. To be back in the midst of that world, not just flitting in for brief meetings or missing receptions because she had something— or rather, some*one*—better to do.

She saw Wren heading toward the paddocks with Foam walking sedately at her side. Grover and Biscuit trotted ahead, racing each other around a thick fir tree. They made a nice picture. A calm picture. Wren was amazing, and the farm was lovely. Gina had always found animals to be sort of stressful, but living here with happy, well-cared-for ones had been a revelation for her. She shook her head, trying to push away her sad emotions. She wasn't really saying good-bye to any of this, since she'd only be an hour away. She could visit Wren all the time and continue some of the photo stories she had started in the area. It would be a small shift—instead of being on the farm most of the time and in the city on occasion, she would have Seattle as her home base. Nothing was really changing in essence, just in degree. Maybe she'd get a cat to keep her company when she moved back to the city. She *had* to move back. She wasn't giving up her dreams for someone else, even if that someone was Wren. She was sure of her decision.

Then, damn it, why was she crying? She had lost some ground with her business, not necessarily in terms of numbers, but in new connections and sponsorships. She needed a constant influx of fresh revenue sources, and she wasn't generating them as quickly as she had when she lived in the city. Wren cared about her success and had always been supportive. She'd understand.

Gina wiped at her tears and called Maia, belatedly realizing how early it was for her night owl friend. Luckily, Maia answered quickly, sounding too cheerful to be someone who had just been rudely awakened.

"They caught him," she said, as soon as Maia said hello.

"Oh, honey, that's great! What a relief. So what happens now?"

"I have to go to the police station, but after that I can go back to normal. Or find a new kind of normal. Maybe I'll check out some apartments today."

"Well, it's wonderful news."

"Yes, it is," Gina agreed.

"And you're crying because..."

"I'm not crying," Gina said, sniffing and wiping the back of her hand across her wet cheek. "Okay, I'm crying a little. I'm just overwhelmed, I suppose. And relieved."

"Sure." Maia paused, then continued. "What did your girlfriend say when you told her?"

"I don't have a...She's not..." Gina sat on the bed and rubbed her temple. She wanted to crawl under the covers again. "I haven't told her yet."

"Really? Why not? She'll be glad to know you're safe."

Gina had no doubt that Wren would be thrilled with the news. She had been protective of Gina and angry about what happened to her from the start, when they had barely known each other. Gina's first day here seemed so long ago now, distant in more ways than temporal.

"I'll tell her right now. Or as soon as I get back from the station." Wren didn't like change. That's why Gina didn't want to tell her. And their relationship would have to change now, but it didn't need to end. They'd adjust, just as Wren had adapted to having Gina here when she had been vocally against the idea at first. Now, Wren wanted her even closer. With her at night, staying until morning. Moving into the house.

Wren was still hurt by her refusal to stay in the house instead of returning to her apartment every night. What she didn't understand was that Gina hated leaving her and walking back to the barn all alone. Climbing into a cold, empty bed and facing the jarring realization that Wren wasn't beside her each morning. But Gina had been smart to keep this distance between them, and now Wren might understand why she had insisted on it. It would make this transition easier to bear, when Gina traveled even farther away after their time together.

"Tell her now. The two of you need to talk this out. Call me later, okay?"

"I will."

Gina said good-bye and ended the call. She took her time getting ready, skipping her morning filming and heading down to the barn later than usual. She wasn't fooling herself into thinking she was moving slowly because she was tired or still processing her news. She was avoiding Wren, hoping she would already be on a horse or teaching a lesson when Gina arrived. She didn't want to talk to Wren because she had a heavy feeling in her stomach that seemed to be saying she was about to lose something important. Even if Wren agreed on adding a little distance to their relationship, Gina was still losing something.

She edged around the barn and saw Wren in the arena, deep in concentration as she trotted Foam diagonally across the arena. Gina stepped back again, leaning against the rough wood of the barn and closing her eyes. She'd go to the station, and then she'd have all the details when she finally talked to Wren. No sense in telling her half a story now, and filling in the rest later. Gina ignored the nagging question in her mind, asking how many half stories she was telling herself, and walked the long way around the barn to get to her car.

❖

Wren twisted in her saddle, looking back toward the barn. She thought she had seen movement, maybe Gina finally coming down to the barn, but no one was there. She sighed and faced forward again, asking Foam for a canter. Their first show of the season was next weekend, and she forced all her worries and wonderings to the back of her mind as she schooled the gray horse. They practiced the more difficult movements he would be required to perform at the show, and he handled everything she asked with quiet ease. She was getting better at shutting out her emotions apparently, because he wasn't overreacting to her signals, and they had a training session that would normally have left her in a cheerful mood all day.

Not today, though. She let Foam walk on a loose rein and rubbed his neck which was damp with sweat. She was losing Gina. She wasn't sure why, or when it would happen, but she felt her slipping away. Their desire for each other certainly wasn't fading—if anything, they were more in tune with each other than they had been at first. And they had fun together, no matter what they were doing. Wren had never imagined she would enjoy wandering around Poulsbo talking about camera angles and which stores would make the best backdrops for an online video, but everything she did with Gina was fun. They were laughing as much as they always had, and talking comfortably, without awkward pauses or arguments.

But something was off. They should have been getting closer, but instead they were flatlining. And they didn't argue or have uncomfortable conversations because they didn't discuss anything more emotionally meaningful than their jobs or concrete things they saw and did. There were no more talks about their childhoods or their dreams—and especially not about their feelings for each other. This relationship was the most significant one in Wren's life, and she felt as if she couldn't discuss it with the one other person who was involved in it.

Wren searched the area around the barn again. Gina had been there some mornings, when she wasn't in Seattle, either filming a video or laying fabric on the ground and arranging bits and pieces of colorful items on it for a photo shoot. Not today. She could be sleeping in for once, since it had been after three in the morning when Gina left her bed, but Wren interpreted her continued absence this morning as a bad omen.

She dismounted and led Foam back to the barn. She had pushed Gina too hard, rushing her into practically moving in. They were staying on the same property, but that didn't mean they had to bypass the natural progression of their relationship, hurrying toward living together just because a moving van wasn't required.

Wren leaned against Foam's warm shoulder, closing her eyes and breathing in the smell of horse and the sweet white pine shavings she had used as bedding in the stalls this morning. She was trying to understand Gina's perspective now, but she didn't feel the same. All she wanted was to grow closer to Gina, and if she was rushing it was because she didn't feel confident in how much of a future they had together. She wasn't even sure about tomorrow. She wanted to make the most of the time they had.

She rode two more horses before she gave in and knocked on the apartment door. When she didn't get an answer, she wandered around the barn and noticed Gina's car was gone. She spent the next hour alternating between wondering why Gina hadn't told her she was going somewhere, since she always had before, and berating herself because Gina didn't need to check in with her. She spent the rest of the morning mentally debating the issue. Would telling Wren where she was going have been common courtesy on Gina's part, or was Wren being too possessive if she expected it? By the time Gina actually did show up, walking down the barn aisle with grocery bags in her hands and a smile on her face, Wren was so worn out from her internal monologues that she felt ready to snap.

"Hey there," Gina said, giving her a quick kiss on the mouth. "I thought I'd make you dinner for a change tonight. I can't promise anything gourmet, but I make a mean curry."

Wren inhaled and exhaled slowly, breathing out her tension and returning Gina's smile. Or repressing her feelings of hurt and anger because she was afraid of pushing Gina further away. Wren told that more cynical side of herself to shut the hell up.

"That sounds good," she said.

Gina shifted the bags into her left hand and ran the other one through her hair, avoiding Wren's eyes. "It's sort of a celebration."

"Really? What's the occasion?" If it was something to do with her subscribers or another incomprehensible internet-related event, Gina would look happier than this, wouldn't she? Instead, she seemed tense.

"The police caught the guy who doxed me."

Wren stood still for a moment, made speechless by Gina's words. She hadn't realized how much her low-key but constant worry about Gina's safety had been weighing on her until the threat evaporated. The words Gina had reported, so long ago, from the threatening comments hovered continuously on the edge of Wren's mind. They were why she went for a casual late-night stroll after Gina left her house each evening, checking the parking area and barn and making sure she didn't see any sign of an intruder. And why she always watched the people around them when they were in public, checking to see if anyone seemed suspicious or overly aware of Gina. She moved forward and grabbed Gina in a tight hug, holding her close, so very glad she was okay.

"God, Gina, that's wonderful. Is there anything you need me to do?"

"No," Gina said with and sigh and a smile, as if she had been unsure of Wren's reaction and was finally relaxing. But how could she have thought Wren would be anything but thrilled?

"I was at the police station today, and I took care of everything I need to right now."

"Good," Wren said. She frowned, finally processing the meaning behind Gina's statement. "Were you at the station checking on the case, and they told you? Or did you know to go there today?"

"They called this morning and asked me to come in," Gina said, putting her hand on Wren's arm. "I was going to tell you before I left. Maia said I should tell you. But you were riding, and I didn't want to break your concentration, especially with the show coming up…"

Maia. Wren had no reason to be jealous of Gina's friend, but she wasn't happy to be the second person Gina wanted to turn to when she had good news to share. Not even the second, really, since she had then gone to the station before coming here and telling Wren, as if she was merely an afterthought. She finally felt a little clarity about the question of whether she was wrong to have been upset at not being told where Gina went today. The answer was no, because she didn't need to be told of her partner's every move. She did, however, expect and deserve to be part of major life occasions, like this one.

To at least be near the top of the list of people who came to Gina's mind when she heard news—good or bad—and wanted to share it.

"That was thoughtful of you," she said, and her voice sounded icy in her ears.

"Wren, don't." Gina set her bags on the ground and came closer, putting her arms around Wren's rib cage and leaning close, turning her head to one side and resting her cheek against Wren's chest. "I wanted to tell you first, but I was afraid of what this means for us. I can move back to the city now. I worked so hard to make my way there, and now I can get back what was taken from me and start growing my following even more. But I don't want to lose you. I want us to make this work."

Wren lifted her hands, wanting to put them on Gina's back and hold her tight. Tell her everything would be okay, and that yes, she was fine with Gina moving back to her life in the city. Wren dropped her hands to her sides. She wasn't going to lie, and she was done hiding her truth from Gina.

She pulled away. "How exactly do you think we can make a long-distance relationship work? How do you see me fitting in with the rest of your life's plan?"

"I'd call it more of a medium-distance relationship." Gina tried to give her a playful smile, but Wren wasn't fooled by it. "Poulsbo is close enough to Seattle that some people make the commute every day for their jobs. We can visit each other all the time. Plus, you've been doing more with the computer, so we could Zoom every—"

"No," Wren said sharply. She was hurt even more by those words than by anything else that had happened. Gina had always seemed to understand her—had made the effort many times to learn about Wren and really pay attention to who she was. How could she have gotten this part of Wren so wrong?

"I will possibly use a computer as a tool for my business, but I will not use one as a substitute for a real relationship. That's... it's not who I am. After all our talks about my lifestyle—hell, even after our jokes about how old-fashioned I am—how could you possibly believe I would want to date a computer screen?"

"Maybe I thought you would compromise your precious values just this once, because you care about me. You know how much city life means to me. You won't make an effort to communicate with me, but you expect me to give up my dreams for you?"

"I don't," Wren said, her voice softening, not because she was ready to kiss and make up, but because she felt the numbness of *It's over* settling deep inside her chest. "I understand that the city became some sort of symbol for what you didn't have growing up. But I don't believe what you're looking for requires a certain size population or that you're doomed to have a second-rate career if you don't live within walking distance of downtown Seattle. I think you could create your dream life anywhere, even here with me."

"And I think you could lighten up and stop shutting out every piece of technology, especially the ones that could have kept us close."

Wren shrugged, as a gesture of surrender, not indifference. "It seems we have very different definitions of the word *close*."

She reached out and laid her palm against Gina's cheek, allowing herself one last sift of her fingers through Gina's silky hair.

"Enjoy your city life, Gina. I hope it truly is everything you want."

CHAPTER EIGHTEEN

I feel like an idiot," Wren said as she stood next to Foam with a brush in her hand and glared at Dianna. "I really don't see the point of this."

Dianna sighed and lowered her phone. "The point is to connect to potential clients. Maybe even make some friends."

"I *have* friends. I'm not particularly fond of one of them right now, but I have others, so she can be replaced." She had plenty of clients, too, in her opinion. After Foam's spectacular Intermediate tests at their show last weekend—not to mention her students' solid performances—she had signed on two more training horses and a new boarder who would be taking lessons twice a week. They were going to seriously cut into her quiet time at the barn. She tried to be her usual cranky self about the intrusions, but she was thriving on the extra work. She had worried that more students would make her less of a teacher, but the opposite was proving to be true. The new riders and horses came with fresh challenges and unique problems to solve. Plus, Wren was secretly glad to have the added distraction. The more time she spent alone, the more she thought incessantly about Gina. At least when other people were around, she could occasionally spend the odd minute or two *not* thinking about her, wondering how she was and what she was doing.

"It might be old-fashioned to attract students through word of mouth, but you have to admit it works. It's how you found me, and Linda, and everyone else who rides here. I only have two empty stalls, anyway, so I don't need to start a worldwide bidding war for them."

"Look, Wren, you're an amazing rider and a talented trainer. You could spend your life here at this farm, teaching the minimum number of lessons you need in order to survive, or you could put a little effort into marketing and become so much more. Instead of reading all those training books in your house, you could write one yourself. And instead of lecturing a bunch of amateur students who aren't as interested in riding theory as you are, you could be sharing those brilliant thoughts you have running through your head with people who really want to hear them."

"Wow." Dianna's words might be an exaggeration of her abilities and potential, but they were the nicest ones she had heard in a long time. They made something stir inside her, too—the same sense of drive she felt every time she stepped into a show ring or started training a challenging horse. "That's really nice of you, Dianna. Thank you."

Dianna snorted. "Don't thank me. I'm basically quoting what Gina said when I talked to her last week. I'm in agreement with her, actually, that you're an idiot."

Way to ruin a moment. Wren tried to ignore the rush of warmth she felt to know Gina was still thinking about her, too. And then the cascade of sadness because she wasn't here anymore. The constant reversals were exhausting. "I didn't know you were still communicating with her."

"Just the one time," Dianna said. "She called to give me the passwords for some accounts she had created for the farm before she left. There's a blog with some posts you wrote and an Instagram account with some of her photos on it. Plus a

YouTube channel, which has a video she made of you riding and some shots of the farm, all set to music. It's lovely, but you can't see it because you don't have a computer."

Wren gestured toward the door with her brush. "I can walk outside and see the farm anytime I want. I can even hum a little tune at the same time if I want ambiance."

Dianna shrugged. "Fine. Pretend you don't care. I just don't think it would hurt to add a blog post or video to those sites now and again, just to see what happens. She put a lot of work into this for you. Certainly more than the apartment she got in return warranted."

Wren shook her head. She had given Gina a place to stay, and she hadn't expected her to do any work in exchange, even though that had been their bargain. Gina had needed to be here. Wren had a feeling Dianna was pushing her because she wanted her to snap out of the listlessness she had been feeling since Gina left. She had perked up at the show, where her competitive instinct had taken over and made her ride like she cared. And she did care that Foam was given the opportunity to show how good he was, and not to have her make him look bad by riding poorly. And she had cared enough to coach her students through their classes. But once the show was over, she returned to the shadow-feeling of not being quite herself.

"You're just trying to make me angry," she said. "It won't work."

Dianna walked over and gave her a quick hug. "I am," she admitted. "I'm worried about you. You're someone who fights for what you believe in, whether it's your tech-free life, your pasture-ornament rescue horses, or your friends. I hate seeing you give up on the most important fight of all."

Wren closed her eyes and took a deep breath, but Gina appeared in her mind, so she opened her eyes again. "I'll film this ridiculous video if we can please stop talking about her."

"Deal, at least for now," Dianna said, holding up her phone again. "Now, just talk to the camera. And try not to look so grouchy."

"You can have one or the other, not both," Wren said as she stepped to Foam's side and ran the brush across his already spotless coat. "I have no idea what to say."

"Come on, Wren," Dianna said with exasperation in her voice. "It's just meant to be a conversational video about horses. Just two weeks ago after my lesson you spent half an hour ranting about leg wraps, which has to be the most boring topic ever. Surely you can manage ten minutes talking about something interesting."

"I did not rant," Wren said, refusing to be manipulated into having a serious conversation with a cell phone. "And it's not a boring topic, it's an important one. Protective boots and leg wraps are meant to be protective, not decorative. Do you know how much damage you can do to tendons and ligaments if they're put on incorrectly?"

"There's the opinionated teacher we all love," Dianna said. She grabbed a tightly wound cotton wrap out of a rack on the wall of the grooming stall and tossed it in Wren's direction. "Here you go. Visual aid."

Wren caught the wrap and put the grooming brush back in its box. "Fine, but go get those horrible stiff boots you bought for Pixie. They're what started my rant in the first place."

❖

Wren managed to fill all the time she had before Dianna's battery died, and she even continued on for a few minutes after. She doubted there was much of an audience for her topic, but at least she got to make Dianna listen to her entire lecture for a second time. That was her revenge for having to film it in the first place. Dianna had left pretty quickly after the video was done, probably wanting to escape before Wren started chatting at length about hoof picks or fly spray, and Wren had spent the rest of her day working with her two new charges.

The afternoon's activities had brought Gina back to the forefront of her mind with painful clarity. She had never really left Wren's thoughts, but Wren had spent the past two weeks trying as hard as she could to push Gina into the background. The day they had fought had been one of the worst of Wren's life, but the two days between that and Gina moving out had been even harder to bear. Wren had been tempted every second to go to the barn apartment and tell Gina she would do whatever it took to keep her in her life. She'd buy a computer, figure out how to Zoom, spend her nights talking to a digital version of the flesh-and-blood woman she had once held in her arms.

Wren locked the feed room door. Time to face the long evening alone. Because she hadn't gone to the apartment either of those nights, no matter how strong the urge had been. She hadn't offered to make any of those compromises, and Gina had left. She had a moving service come this time, and Wren had taken Jasper for a ride along the beach when she saw the truck pull in, staying far from the barn until it drove away again, taking Gina and her computers and her cameras with it.

Wren left the barn, but instead of going back to her house, she turned in the opposite direction and walked over to the apartment's staircase. She hadn't been inside since the first day when she had helped move in Gina's furniture and boxes. After today's reminders of Gina, she foolishly wanted to feel closer to her, even though she knew it would only make her hurt more. She put her hand on the rough railing and climbed the stairs, wondering how different her life would be right now if she had come here two weeks ago, and if Gina had taken her back and agreed to try having a facsimile of a relationship with her. Would she feel happier now? Or would she feel lonelier—if that was even possible—being able to see Gina, but not truly sharing their lives together?

Wren got to the landing and leaned her back against the door for a moment, looking out over the bay, with its view of trees and mountains, and a sliver of Poulsbo. This was the view Gina had when she was here, and Wren had thought Gina was starting to appreciate this serene space nearly as much as Wren did. But maybe she had looked out the window and had only seen the curved, glowing dome over the artificially lit Seattle, visible across the Sound now, as dusk settled in. Wren thought it was beautiful from a distance and exciting to visit, but she appreciated the distance between here and there, and the silence and peace of her farm. Maybe Gina had looked at the light with longing, wanting to be there, and not here.

What view did she have now? Maybe she was in a high-rise, with the bustling city spread out before her, or in one of Seattle's tightly packed residential areas with narrow streets and tall oak trees. Wren hoped she was happy, wherever she was. Happy and content in the life she claimed was the only possible option for her.

Letting her go, letting her escape to that life, was Wren's only option, really. She had been halfway to the barn the night before Gina left, prepared to sell her low-tech soul for the chance to be with the woman she loved, when that word had stopped her in her tracks. She loved Gina. What wouldn't she give up or change to be with the woman she loved? What compromises wouldn't she be willing to make?

She had turned around and gone back home, knowing the answers to those questions in her heart. If she had merely liked Gina, if her feelings had stopped at being attracted to her and enjoying her company, then she would have gone to the apartment. She would have made some alterations to her strict rules about what she allowed in her life and her home, and she would have tried a relationship on Gina's terms. It might have been exciting in its way, with weekends full of sex and laughter, unmarred by the usual silly arguments, minor irritations, and hurt feelings that would naturally be part of living with another person in a full-time relationship.

But she wouldn't compromise on love. Dianna had been right when she said Wren was someone who fought wholeheartedly and without backing down for the things that truly mattered to her. One of those things was love—she had learned how high it was on the list in the split second it had taken her to turn around that night. She couldn't handle anything less than a full life together with Gina—*together*, in every sense of the world, from where they lived to the direction they wanted their future to take. She wasn't fighting to keep their relationship going in a diluted form. Instead, she fought with herself daily to keep from doing anything that would keep Gina from her goal of finding happiness in city living.

Wren unlocked the apartment door and walked in, gasping softly as she looked around the transformed space. She had thought her cleaning session had gotten the old place looking about as good as it ever would, but Gina had worked magic in here. Although her belongings were gone, she had left behind a few items that she had obviously made just for this space. Wren could barely recognize them as what she had considered to be junk when they bought them at the antique store.

When Gina had told her she was going to be painting, Wren had worried she'd cover the old wood plank walls with some garish color, but instead she had given the wood a pale, distressed look with brushed-on stains. Wren recognized one of the darker tones as the one still streaked on Grover's side, which was fading about as quickly as Wren's memories of

Gina. Gauzy curtains, the color of aged linen, covered the windows with just enough opacity to provide some privacy, but not enough to keep out the sunrise. The plain wood window frames were painted green to match the carpet, and the little cabinet they had found in Poulsbo was a cheerful yellow next to the kitchen window. The drawers were pulled out at different distances, making a stepladder effect, each level bristling with several tiny pots of herbs.

The effect was rustic and comfortable. Gina hadn't tried to recreate a city apartment style or a modern look but had kept a rural, farmhouse feeling. Wren stood in the center of the room, seeing Gina everywhere she looked. The beauty she had inside was reflected in the space she had created here. Someone who truly hated it here, who didn't appreciate the peace and beauty of the farm, could never have made something so perfectly suited to it.

Wren sighed. She might be reading too much into the apartment's decor, trying to see Gina's growing love for this place made tangible on the walls and counters when all Gina had done was make a few simple craft projects. She spotted a large package on the kitchen counter, wrapped in plain brown paper. A cream-colored tag with her name lettered on it in elegant script was tied on with twine.

She just held the bundle for a few moments, guessing what she would find inside. She wasn't sure she was ready to see such glaring reminders of Gina, let alone hang them on her walls in her home, where she would walk by them every day and be reminded of what she had lost. Eventually she couldn't stand waiting any longer, and she untied the twine, carefully peeling open the tape on the paper. She set the three photos side by side on the counter.

Gina had enlarged the photos with isolated shots of Foam and Wren. They were set in plain black frames that matched the others in Wren's house. They had such a sense of vitality and movement to them that Wren could almost feel Foam springing off the ground and into his next step. She ran a finger around one of the frames, tracing the black-painted wood and connecting to Gina, who had put time and care into making this gift.

Wren mentally shook herself and pulled her hand back. This was why she had avoided the apartment and everything else that reminded her of Gina. The bucket she used as a table when filming in the barn, the rolling chair she had sat in when they were in the office. Her side of the bed, where she had dozed but never really slept.

The herbs were desperate for water, so Wren picked up the small cabinet full of their pots and tucked the photos under her other arm. She used her foot to shut the door behind her as she left. She meant to go back to her house, but had to make a detour to the barn first. She couldn't ignore the present Gina had given her. It had already been so long, Gina probably thought she didn't like the photos or didn't care enough to thank her. She probably wouldn't guess the truth, that Wren found it too painful to be reminded of her and had stayed far away from the apartment until tonight.

She set her armload of stuff on the desk and picked up the phone. As much as she professed to hate telephones, she had memorized Gina's number and dialed it now. When she had first met Gina and heard about her internet career, she had assumed she'd be the type who couldn't even set her phone down without having an anxiety attack. Now, though, she knew Gina well enough that she wasn't surprised when her call went to voice mail. If Gina was working or online talking to a friend, she wouldn't break to answer a call. Then again, she might have recognized Wren's number and chosen not to answer.

Or she might be on a date.

Wren stumbled through her first words of her message, shaken by the thought even though Gina had every right to date someone else.

"Anyway, I wanted to thank you for the photos. They're beautiful, and you did a perfect job of framing them." She paused but pushed on again quickly in case the recording cut her off. She didn't want to call back and have to go through this again. "I know we both were aware of the way things would end for us, with you going back to the twenty-first century and me staying here in the nineteenth, but I guess I didn't realize how hard it would be until it actually happened. I'm sorry things were tense between us at the end. I…"

I what? *I'll talk to you later?* Wren wouldn't call her again. *I love you?* She couldn't say that.

"I hope you're happy. Good-bye, Gina."

She hung up the phone and picked up the photos and herbs again, walking through the darkening evening to her house. She supposed it hadn't really mattered what she said in her message. In the end, *I love you* and *I hope you're happy* meant the same thing.

CHAPTER NINETEEN

Gina parked her rental car in front of a rust-colored house with yellow trim. The wide front porch had columns framing the front door, also painted yellow and supporting a high-peaked gable roof. She sat in her idling vehicle under a large leafy tree that looked as if it was dripping vines onto the sidewalk. They swayed in a light breeze, just brushing across the roof of her car. The Berry Hill neighborhood reminded her of Beacon Hill. It was far enough outside the city of Nashville to feel homey, but close enough to have the big-city sense of diversity and quirkiness.

She felt uncomfortably like a stalker as she waited to summon the courage to call Maia. She hadn't let her friend know she was coming, partly because she hadn't made the decision until just this morning. She didn't want to show up on Maia's doorstep in person and unannounced, without giving her at least a chance to tell Gina to go away. She was pretty sure she didn't have to worry, since Maia seemed to have a much fuller real-world life than Gina did, and to be less awkward when it came to in-person relationships. She had friends she met in Nashville for drinks and game nights balanced alongside her online relationships. Gina had the latter, but no one she considered really close in the former category. She had a quick thought of Dianna, Nick and his boys, and Linda flash through her mind, but she dismissed them. They didn't count because they were Wren's friends, not hers, although she could easily imagine spending time with them if things had turned out differently with Wren. She hadn't had the same trouble talking to them, making jokes and laughing with them, as she had when she tried to talk to...

Oh. She couldn't remember the last time she had really tried to connect with someone deeply enough to be pushed out of her comfort zone. In Seattle, she had made small talk with her landlord's family, or with people she encountered in shops. She had carried on careful conversations at PR events, always with the awareness that these people were her peers, but also her competition. She was comfortable carrying on those low-risk conversations, but until she had gone to Poulsbo, she hadn't put herself on the line enough to take a chance of emotional pain.

She had been shy as a child and teen, when she had attempted to make friends and had met only teasing and bullying, but she was an adult now. No longer a child whose self-esteem and confidence were dependent on approval from others. No longer someone who wanted someone—*anyone*—to like her, but a woman who recognized which people and opinions really mattered to her. She had held on to those habits, though, of holding herself apart and not opening herself up to possible rejection. Now, not only was she less likely to face rejection than she had been in her small-minded and afraid-of-anyone-different community, but she was strong enough to handle it if it came.

Yet here she was, hiding in her car outside her good friend's house. A friend who had repeatedly asked her to visit and had even offered to come to Seattle. Gina had always been concerned that their easy friendship wouldn't survive the transition from virtual to live, and she had been afraid of losing it. Did she really think Maia was going to tell her to leave? Close her curtains and turn out the lights to fool Gina into thinking she wasn't home? She hated thinking about how much she had missed by pushing other people away.

And Wren. Even worse was imagining if she hadn't been herself with Wren, rolling her eyes at Wren's cranky act, moving onto her farm where they would be in close contact, and refusing to avoid her. No matter how hurt she had been when their relationship ended, she would much rather accept the pain if it meant she could keep her memories of their time together.

Gina got out of the car and slammed her door, angry with those stupid kids from her childhood for still living in her head, and even more irate with herself for letting them. Finished with her low-key venting, she took a deep breath and filled her lungs with Tennessee air—sweeter and muggier than Seattle's. She liked what she had seen of the city so far, and she might have been tempted to consider a move here since she still didn't have a new place to live in Seattle. No matter how sweet and floral the air was here, though, it couldn't compare to the Pacific Northwest, where Wren's breath was close enough to add to the molecules Gina inhaled.

Gina sighed, letting the sadness of her Wren-less life move over and through her. She had learned to stop fighting the feeling when it came, or it would build and threaten to incapacitate her. She had to accept the sorrow. Learn to live with it. Once the acute hurt had eased a little, she held up her phone and called Maia, centering Maia's front porch on her screen.

"Hi, Gina. What's—Hey, is that my house?"

"Yes, I..." Gina was about to explain her unexpected arrival, but she heard a shriek and the image of Maia on her screen was replaced by a sudden tilting blur, apparently a view of Maia's rug as her phone tumbled to the floor. Then she was outside, pulling Gina into a hug before she had a chance to end their call and put her phone away.

Maia stepped back, and questions tumbled out of her. "When did you get here? Why didn't you tell me you were coming? How long are you staying?"

Gina opened her mouth to try to answer everything, but Maia was peering in the car. "Where's your luggage? Let's go inside and talk."

"I was going to get a hotel," Gina said. She obviously didn't need to be worried about whether Maia was happy to see her, but a stop-by visitor and a drop-in houseguest were two very different things.

Maia put her hands on her hips. "If you tell me that Wren is hiding somewhere in this car, and the two of you want the privacy of a hotel room, I'll help you find one. If you still haven't made up with her, then you're staying here so I can talk some sense into you."

Gina blinked back a sudden pang of tears at the thought of how much fun it would have been to come here with Wren. She and Maia had gotten along so well on the phone—Wren's nemesis in the world of communication—that Gina was sure they'd have enjoyed each other's company even more in person. She shook her head. "No lectures, okay? Besides, she's the one who ended it. If anyone needs an infusion of sense, it's her not me."

"Oh, *right*," Maia said, drawing out the syllables. "She told you to leave her farm and go back to Seattle and after you begged to be able to move in with her. I forgot. That bitch."

Gina shook her head, trying to laugh at Maia's sarcasm, but failing. Her face must have reflected how much the memory of her missteps hurt because Maia's expression softened.

"No lectures," she promised. "For at least an hour."

Maia led her inside and gave her a tour of the modest, three-bedroom house. Gina recognized some things from Maia's videos and photos, both areas she used as backdrops for filming and objects she had featured in Instagram stories. The experience was a little bizarre as Gina had traveled halfway across the country to a home—a whole state, really—where she'd never been before, and yet everything around seemed familiar. It helped make her feel relaxed and at home, and she made up the sofa bed in the spare room while Maia called her husband.

"All set," Maia said when she came back into the room just as Gina put a blue and green striped case over a pillow and laid it at the head of the bed. "Kirk will meet us downtown after work, and we can have dinner. It'll be nice enough to take a walk around the neighborhood after we eat, and then we can go get some drinks. Our favorite pub has open mic every weeknight."

"Sounds like fun," Gina said, forcing a smile even though her mind had returned to Wren, as it always did when she was making plans and wishing Wren could be part of them.

"We have another couple hours before we need to meet him, so let me finish editing the video I was working on when you called. Then we can head into the city and do some shopping. There's a great music store, and an indie bookstore I know you'll love. And we can get coffee at a café that makes the hugest cookies." She paused and looked over her shoulder at Gina as she led the way into the extra room she and her husband had converted into a studio. "How long are you staying? We'll need at least a month if I'm going to be able to show you everything you need to see."

Gina laughed. "I'm flying back on Sunday. I'd love to stay longer, but I really need to find an apartment. The extended stay hotel I'm at is expensive, and it's not even in a good location. I'm practically under the planes taking off from SeaTac."

Maia sat down at her desk. "Sunday is too soon. I'll edit fast, and we'll see how much of Nashville we can cram in before you have to go." She waved around the room. "Go ahead and explore whatever you want. I know you want to because I'm planning to investigate your filming stuff when I come visit you in Seattle."

Gina had to admit she was curious to see another influencer's studio. At first, she wandered around the room, examining items that were on tables or counters, but eventually she gave in to temptation and started prowling through drawers, comparing Maia's filming equipment and photo props to her own. After her self-guided tour, she had a wish list of items she'd like to have in her own studio someday, as well as a few ideas of things she could get in Seattle that Maia might be able to use. She'd send her a thank-you box for letting her stay as soon as she got home. The prospect of being back in Seattle made her feel a little queasy. Hunting for an affordable—yet still habitable—apartment was going to be stressful. Finding a place to live in by herself when Wren was so close, but still out of reach, was going to be brutal.

"Are you alphabetizing my backdrops?" Maia's voice interrupted Gina's circular thoughts. She had just folded a square of deep red satin and tucked it in place near the bottom of the pile she had in front of her. She hadn't realized what she was doing since it had become a habit in just three weeks for her to seek out busywork to occupy her hands and mind when she started thinking too long about Wren.

"Of course not," Gina said indignantly. "That would be ridiculous."

She picked up a yard of red buffalo plaid flannel and placed it under the satin. "I organize by color first, then by weight of the fabric. Brocades, fleeces, and so on are on the bottom, and silks and lace are on top."

"That's not ridiculous at all," Maia said with a laugh. She glanced at her computer screen. "Hey, look. Your girlfriend just posted another video."

"She's not my...she what?" Gina dropped the navy fabric on top of the pile and went to look over Maia's shoulder. "Are you sure it's not the montage video I made of her farm before I left?"

"No. She's posted three of her own, where she talks about horse things. I have no idea what any of it means, but she's hilarious. She has such a droll sense of humor." Maia frowned at her. "I figured you'd be watching her channels. Are you really over her? Because the two of you make a gorgeous couple."

"Wren has made three videos?" Gina was having a hard time processing that piece of information, let alone answering Maia's other questions. She had given Dianna the information for Wren's online sites, but she had doubted the passwords would ever be used. And now Wren was posting *videos*? She hadn't bothered to check Wren's YouTube channel because she didn't think anything new would be on it. And if she had wanted to watch Wren riding over and over—which she *didn't*...at least not very often—she had the original footage on her laptop.

But there was Wren, gesturing and chatting as if she had been in front of a camera since she was old enough to talk. She was discussing topics she seemed to take very seriously, but Maia was right about her humor—her wit blended with her sardonic expressions made a very appealing combination. Gina barely noticed when Maia got up and gently pushed Gina into her chair in front of the computer. Gina somehow managed to drag her gaze away from Wren's face and scroll through the comments. She didn't have a huge following, of course, but she had a decent number of views and comments for a new channel that she was likely doing absolutely nothing to promote.

She was actually responding to comments, too. The earliest responses were probably written by Dianna, Gina thought, but soon enough Wren's voice and passion were present. She had lengthy threads with a few different people who seemed as fascinated by the topic as she was, including a man from the Netherlands and a woman from Germany.

Gina wasn't sure how she felt. Pride was close to the top of the list, because Wren had really stepped out of her comfort zone. She felt proud of herself, too, since without her work on the channel, this side of Wren might not have been showcased like it deserved to be.

Mostly, she felt sad. Plain and simple sadness. She missed Wren with an ache that started in her chest and spread outward until every part of her felt it. She wanted to be angry, to whine about how Wren was willing to go online now, in front of strangers, but she hadn't been willing to give a partially screen-based relationship with Gina a chance.

She knew that anger would be misplaced, though. Wren had powerful feelings about the kinds of things that mattered to her, and a relationship would definitely be one of them. Her online presence would be far down the list, and Wren wouldn't care if virtual relationships were diluted by distance and a screen. She would care if her love was treated with the same indifference.

Which is exactly what Gina had done when she offered Wren the occasional visit and Zoom session instead of real love.

Gina wiped her damp cheek with the back of her hand.

When had she started thinking the word *love* in connection with Wren? She sighed. She couldn't pinpoint a date, but she knew the emotion had been behind whichever words she had been using for a long time.

Maia put her arm around Gina's shoulders and rested her cheek on the top of Gina's head. "Oh, honey, you've got it bad, don't you?"

Gina nodded.

"So tell her." Maia tapped the screen. "Put a comment down here. *Hey, baby, I miss you.*"

Gina laughed, trying to imagine Wren's reaction to a comment like that. "Not through a computer," she said. "It'd have to be in person, or she wouldn't believe I understood her at all. And it's too late, anyway."

She had made the exact same mistake when she suggested they move their relationship to the virtual realm to give her a chance to move farther away than the apartment. She knew how much she had hurt Wren because she had offered something so alien to who Wren was as a substitute for what they had been building between them. She had thought she was making the right choice, though. She had to stay true to herself, too, didn't she?

"It's never too late," Maia said, pulling away and dragging another chair close to the computer.

"Besides," Gina went on, unconvinced by Maia's last comment, "nothing has changed. I need to live in the city. It's always been my dream."

"Yeah, you've mentioned that before."

Gina frowned at the skepticism in Maia's voice. "You sound like you don't believe me."

"Oh, I believe you. I just don't know if the actual city is the dream. I think getting away from your old town was the dream, and it was a good one to have. Seattle was just the most opposite place you could imagine, so you turned it into a goal."

"Wren said practically the same thing, that the city was a symbol."

Maia grinned. "See? Brilliant minds, as they say."

Gina crossed her arms over her chest. "Well, I think you're both wrong, and I'm the one who should know what my own goals are. And living in the city is the top one."

"Okay," Maia said with a shrug. "Why, exactly?"

Gina was about to mention diversity, but she had met people from different ethnic and racial backgrounds among Wren's friends in Poulsbo, so she focused instead on what set Seattle apart. "Most of all, it's important for my career. The connections I can make there are unbeatable in the Northwest, and I was surrounded by other influencers when I lived close to downtown." Maia still didn't look convinced, so Gina branched into similar arguments Maia had used when she had tried to get Gina to move to Nashville. "Plus, the arts scene is fantastic. Operas, plays, the symphony. SAM, the art museum, has world-renowned exhibitions."

Maia poked her in the ribs. "If you can name the last opera you saw, I will drop the subject right now and never bring it up again."

Gina was going to make one up, but nothing came to mind. "They're expensive. But the point is, I could go to one if I wanted."

"You could watch one online for free or just a couple dollars. Have you done that?"

Gina tried to take a calming breath. "Let's just forget about the opera. The point is, there are opportunities in the city. It's energizing and exciting. And it's crowded, so you can be anonymous, which is very freeing. It's so close to Poulsbo that Wren and I could have seen each other all the time, but she wouldn't even give us a chance."

"Maybe she wanted a girlfriend and not an occasional visitor."

"And maybe I wasn't prepared to be that committed," Gina said, but the words sounded hollow to her. She sighed, feeling her shoulders sag under the weight of honesty. "Or maybe I was scared of our relationship because letting go of Seattle felt like I'd be abandoning myself and everything I worked so hard to make happen in my life, throwing away my chance at a really amazing career."

Maia reached over and clicked a bookmark, opening Gina's Instagram on the screen. The partial photos of Foam and Wren appeared and made her breath hitch the same way it always did when she saw Wren, or even just the edge of her boot.

"I've been following you for a long time, even before we became friends," Maia continued. "If I'd noticed that your content seemed stifled or weaker because you weren't in Seattle, I'd tell you. But if anything, you seemed to expand in the types of posts you did, like you were more inspired. Your photos are even better, too. What might be more important to you, but shouldn't be, is that your numbers have been steadily increasing. Cities can be very inspiring, but so can beautiful natural places. I think something there—Poulsbo or Wren or both of them—gave you a fresh perspective. Besides, you said it yourself that Poulsbo is close to Seattle. Even if you lived there, you could go to..."

She paused as Gina glared at her, daring her to mention the damned opera again. "You could go to the symphony whenever you wanted. I'm sure you do that all the time. But it would be better, because it would be you and Wren sharing it together."

"Look," Maia continued, putting her hand on Gina's shoulder and giving her a squeeze. "There's something special about you and about the way you communicate with words and pictures. You don't have to follow the route everyone else is taking, going after the same sponsors every other micro-influencer is courting. The really big names in our business make their own paths. Keep making connections with Seattle businesses if you want, but don't let them or any other influencers define your brand or your journey."

Gina thought back to the way ideas had flowed through her in Poulsbo. She had been forced to be more creative because she wanted to keep from exposing her location in pictures. She hadn't been able to rely on sharing photos and videos from her backyard or the block around her apartment. She had relished the way her more expansive thinking was changing her content, but she hadn't considered letting it change the way she approached marketing, too. She had been convinced she needed to follow the crowd when it came to the money side of her business, even though it had never felt comfortable or right for her.

She sighed. Even if she convinced herself that she could live in Poulsbo, she wasn't sure if Wren would ever be willing to take her back. The more time she spent away from her, the more she was starting to see that maybe a new dream had replaced the old one. She might be too late to make this one come true, though.

Maia seemed to sense that Gina's ability to keep up this conversation was nearing an end. She closed her browser and patted Gina on the knee. "Enough sad talk. We'll feed you some Nashville barbecue and show you around. Tomorrow, when you're more rested, we can do some brainstorming for both of our careers. By the time Sunday comes, you'll be rested and ready to do what you need to do to make yourself happy. And I'm expecting you to get up and sing your favorite aria at the open mic."

Gina swatted at her, laughing and releasing some of the tension she held inside. Maia made it sound easy—find out what would make her happy, and go get it. And when Gina thought about true happiness, it wasn't tall buildings or crowds of people she pictured. It was, quite simply, Wren.

Chapter Twenty

Wren flicked the black mesh fly sheet over Foam's back and smoothed it into place. She buckled it in front of his chest and under his belly before fishing a crumbling treat out of her pocket and holding it on her open palm for him to nibble.

Maybe she should do a video on her homemade horse cookies. Since her earliest days spent learning to bake and cook, she had experimented on horse treats until she found a few that were irresistible, in Calypso's opinion. She had added dog treat recipes to her repertoire once she had moved out of her parents' house and could have them as pets.

Wren sighed and unclipped the crossties from Foam's halter. She led him down the barn aisle and outside into the sunshine. She wasn't sure how she felt about this new habit of hers—an affliction she had obviously caught from Gina—to turn every thought she had while taking care of her horses into a potential topic for a video. On the one hand, she had always had plenty to say on just about every aspect of equine care and training, but she had rarely had people around her who were as interested in discussing them as she was. Even her most horse-obsessed students had limits to their patience when it came to debates about riding theory or musings on horse products and practices. She had needed to widen her search to encompass the entire world, but she had managed to find a few people online who were as intrigued by odd and interesting equine issues as she was.

On the other hand, though…computers.

Wren wasn't happy with having computers take up even a tiny corner of her universe. She wasn't sure if she was selling out to the insidious appeal of these technological black holes that just might—Gina's and Dianna's jokes aside—steal her soul, or if she was making a positive step toward being more open-minded and adaptable. For now, she was comfortable letting the conundrum simmer in her mind while she made a few cautious steps into the online world, always willing to pull back if necessary.

What she *wasn't* comfortable with was the way any thought of videos or computers led to thoughts of Gina. She had been gone for almost a month, and Wren had expected the pain of losing her to be fading by now. She should be moving on to some other stage, shouldn't she? Anger or acceptance or anything less awful than the sadness she felt. She was functioning and getting on with her life, but she would always be aware of how much richer and more fun that life would be if Gina was sharing it with her.

She slipped Foam's halter off his head and shut the paddock gate. She could probably make things a little easier for herself if she made a few changes. Banish computers completely, which had worked just fine for her since she had done it the first time as a teenager. Take down the photos from Gina she had hung in her house—in her bedroom of all places, which was just about the stupidest thing she had ever done.

It was almost as if she didn't want to move on.

She started back toward the barn when Grover suddenly tilted his head to one side, staring toward the front of the property. He took off in the direction of the driveway, and Biscuit tore after him.

Wren sighed. Company. She didn't have any lessons scheduled, so it must be one of the owners out to ride or discuss their horse's training progress with her. This was happening more and more frequently, since the three new clients she had taken on after the show had increased by another three who had contacted her because of her videos. Word of mouth and the internet were tied so far. Wren wasn't pleased with either one of them since these new clients were seriously cutting into her brooding-over-Gina time.

She followed the sound of Biscuit's excited yips and halted on the edge of the gravel lot when she saw Gina's car. The moment too accurately mirrored the one from weeks earlier, when Gina had first arrived. Now, though, she got immediately out of her car and was hugging Grover while Biscuit raced in circles around them.

Wren wanted nothing more than to join the pack and take Gina in her arms, but she hung back, uncertain what Gina's arrival meant, or what she wanted it to mean.

Gina finally stood up and faced her. Wren remained silent, waiting for her to speak, to explain why she was here. Gina took a couple false starts, as if she wasn't quite sure what to say, either.

"You fixed his hair," Gina said with a smile, ruffling the fur at Grover's neck, where she had attempted to cut out the spilled glue.

"Yes," Wren said, biting back the urge to make a joke or a sarcastic comment. She was surprised by how easy it would have been for her to slide back into effortless banter with Gina. Talking to her had always felt very natural, in a way Wren had never experienced before with anyone else. It almost felt as if she had merely gone to the store and was back, not as if she had left for good. Almost.

Gina's smile faded, and she crossed the distance between them. She halted just out of reach. "Wren, I'm so sorry. I know I've made a mess of things. Of us. I was hoping we could talk."

The inflection on her last sentence made it a question, but it took a moment for Wren to register. She was supposed to say something now, but she had no idea what it should be. *Okay, I'd like that*? Or her old standby *Get the hell off my property*?

"Fine. Talk." Wren cringed inwardly. Apparently she was taking the caveman approach of *You talk, me listen*. Still, the bare words were all she could manage when her thoughts and emotions were racing chaotically through her mind, not to mention her desire to touch Gina and make sure she was really standing there. Her brain didn't have enough energy leftover for verbal finesse.

Gina visibly took a deep breath before she spoke. She looked down at Grover, who was sitting next to her and leaning against her leg. "I've missed you," she said. "I knew I would, but I didn't realize how much. I thought the most important thing for me was to get my life back to the way it was before I came here, and I didn't stop long enough to notice that I had stopped missing most of it once I got here. The important things, like my career and being creative, are part of me, no matter where I am. The rest of it just didn't matter as much as it had before because I was here with you."

Wren scuffed at the gravel with her boot, and Biscuit pounced on the moving pebbles. "You left as soon as you had the chance, though. You didn't seem to have any doubt about where you wanted to be."

Gina spread her hands as if in surrender, then dropped them back to her sides. "The dream was too ingrained for me to just ignore it until I got my city life back and understood just how empty it was. I thought being in Seattle was the only way to be successful, but I was wrong." She paused and looked at Wren. "You said the city was a symbol, and I've been thinking a lot about what the city really means to me. What it stands for. When I was younger, people looked at me and found something to mock, so I wanted to be where people wouldn't even bother to look at me in the first place. Being an anonymous person in a sea of hundreds of thousands of others seemed safe."

Wren shook her head and took a tentative half step forward. "Hiding who you are can't be the answer."

"I know that now, but when I was a kid, protecting myself was the priority. I couldn't understand that what I really needed was to find people who looked at me and liked what they saw. I found that when I connected with others online who had similar interests and hobbies, but I found it even more here with you, where even though we're very different in some ways, we still respect and find value in each other."

Wren frowned. She had loved the same thing about their relationship because no matter how much they teased or didn't relate to certain aspects of each other's lives, they had never expected the other to change significant parts of their identities. Until Gina had said she was moving away. "I didn't feel respected when you offered me, of all people, an online relationship."

Gina winced, as if the words caused her pain. "You're right. You said then that I didn't seem to get you at all if I thought you would accept those terms, but you were wrong about that. I knew you wouldn't want us to connect that way, but I was desperate enough to try. I wanted my old dream back, but I also wanted to keep hold of my new one. You."

She continued before Wren responded, as if she needed to say the rest of her thoughts out loud as quickly as she could. "I like Seattle and what it has to offer. It's a great city, and

I'll always want to be close to a place like it, where so many unique people and places all come together. But I don't need to live there, copying other people's blueprints for a successful career. I can be happy being close enough to it to visit every once in a while, and I could be happy if I exchanged it for another city. But, you…Wren, I love you. I don't want to live someplace else and only see you part of the time, and I could never find someone to replace you."

Wren knew more would need to be said about this, and she still ached from being apart, but right now she desperately needed to feel close to Gina. She walked over to Gina and wrapped her arms around her, threading one hand through her hair and putting the other on her lower back, pulling her close. Gina looped her arms tightly around Wren's neck. Neither seemed willing to let the other go, but Wren pulled back enough to be able to look Gina in the eyes.

"I don't understand why you ever thought you needed to follow the crowd to be a success," she said, resting her forehead against Gina's. "From the first moment we met, I could tell you were unlike anyone else I'd ever known. And, like your followers, I couldn't take my eyes off you. I love you, too, Gina. If I didn't, I might have been tempted to try things your way, at least for a while."

Gina shook her head. "I'm glad you said no. It wouldn't have worked." She moved her hands down until her palms were resting on Wren's chest, just below her collarbones. "Although it might have been a little bit fun. You're really sexy on the screen."

Wren laughed. "Even when I'm talking about leg wraps or bridles?"

"Meh," Gina said, with a small shrug. "It helps if I mute you."

Wren pulled out of her arms and gave her a playful swat

on the hip. "I can't believe you just said that. Way to ruin a special moment."

It hadn't, though. If anything, the return to lightheartedness made the moment seem even more real. Laughter and joy were a big part of what they had had together, and Wren was ready to explore whether or not they could get it back again.

Gina laughed, as if she felt the same way. "I really can't believe you're making online videos. Welcome to the grid, Wren."

Wren rubbed the back of her neck. Her lifestyle was a confusing blend of old and new right now, and she had a feeling Gina's return if she really was planning to stay—was a sign of more upheaval to come. "My house is still off-limits," she said. "It's an oasis of solar power and limited EM waves, but I've made a few compromises in the barn. If you want to see, I'll show you."

Gina nodded and tentatively reached for Wren's hand as they walked. Wren took the opportunity of paying attention to where she was going and not looking directly at Gina to ask the question nagging at her mind.

"What now, Gina? Are you still wanting to split your time between your new place and here? Because I don't think I can—"

Gina squeezed her hand and made her stop. "My new place is a hotel. I was sort of hoping I could come back. Maybe rent the barn apartment or something? Anything, as long as we have a chance to be together."

"That might be a problem," Wren said, trying to sound reluctant even though her heart seemed to be doing some sort of celebratory dance in her chest. She might need to get to a hospital if it didn't settle down. She stopped at the foot of the staircase and turned to face Gina, gesturing with her head toward the apartment above them. "I've turned this place into my social media studio. I'm even thinking of using the kitchen for filming a video about making horse treats."

"Well, since this place is taken, maybe I could move into the house." Gina said the words with a shrug, as if they didn't matter, but Wren could read her expression well enough to know how much they did. She leaned forward and kissed her, moving her lips slowly across Gina's and feeling an overwhelming sense of rightness.

She rested her forehead against Gina's. "I think the dogs and I can squeeze you in. I'll put a basket on the front patio, though, and you'll have to leave all your tech in there before you come inside."

She started up the staircase, hearing Gina's laughter behind her. "I'll leave some of it, but not all. I'll need my laptop, my phone, my—"

Wren paused on the landing and held up her hand. "I think you're misunderstanding what the word *need* means."

Gina grabbed the front of Wren's shirt and pulled her into a kiss that was fierce with longing and relief. A brush of her tongue made Wren open her mouth, welcoming Gina home without any lingering hesitation.

Gina moved an inch away. "I believe I know exactly what the word *need* means."

Wren grinned at her. "That was an impressive vocabulary lesson. I have a few other words I'd like you to define for me, too. Later, though. For now, welcome to Lindley Farm's IT department."

She stepped back and opened the door with a flourish. Gina stepped over the threshold and looked around.

"Cozy," she said with a choking sound as if she was fighting back laughter.

"I don't want to get too comfortable here," Wren said. The

room was bare, just as it had been when Gina left, except for a folding chair and Gina's old upturned bucket.

"You actually got a computer," Gina said, gesturing at the small laptop perched on the bucket.

"The cheapest one they had," Wren admitted. "The more expensive ones came with more features."

"And you want to enjoy it as little as possible," Gina finished for her, finally giving up on restraint and laughing.

"Exactly," Wren said, with a smile. "You get me." She hesitated, then switched back to a more serious tone. "I'll never be a big fan of technology. I think it has the ability to distract us from life. Filter it, and separate us from the world around us. But I do like communicating, sharing ideas, and learning new things. I'm struggling with how to incorporate this new stuff into my life without losing sight of myself, but I really do appreciate this new world you've shown me."

Gina smiled and placed her palm on Wren's cheek. "We're good for each other," she said. "I really believe that."

Wren nodded, unable to put into words how much it meant to have Gina back and to see hope for a future with them together, sharing their lives in new and unexpected ways. She kissed her again, letting her body communicate her love in a way nothing else could.

About the Author

Karis Walsh lives in the Pacific Northwest, where she finds inspiration for the settings of her contemporary romances and romantic intrigues. She was a Golden Crown Literary Award winner with *Tales from Sea Glass Inn*, and her novels have been shortlisted for a Lambda Literary Award and a Forward INDIES award. She can usually be found reading with a cat curled on her lap, hiking with a dog at her side, or playing her viola with both animals hiding under the bed. Contact her at kariswalsh@gmail.com.

Books Available From Bold Strokes Books

Secret Agent by Michelle Larkin. CIA Agent Peyton North embarks on a global chase to apprehend rogue agent Zoey Blackwood, but her commitment to the mission is tested as the sparks between them ignite and their sizzling attraction approaches a point of no return. (978-1-63555-753-4)

Journey to Cash by Ashley Bartlett. Cash Braddock thought everything was great, but it looks like her history is about to become her right now. Which is a real bummer. (978-1-63555-464-9)

Liberty Bay by Karis Walsh. Wren Lindley's life is mired in tradition and untouched by trends until social media star Gina Strickland introduces an irresistible electricity into her off-the-grid world. (978-1-63555-816-6)

Scent by Kris Bryant. Nico Marshall has been burned by women in the past wanting her for her money. This time, she's determined to win Sophia Sweet over with her charm. (978-1-63555-780-0)

Shadows of Steel by Suzie Clarke. As their worlds collide and their choices come back to haunt them, Rachel and Claire must figure out how to stay together and, most of all, stay alive. (978-1-63555-810-4)

The Clinch by Nicole Disney. Eden Bauer overcame a difficult past to become a world champion mixed martial artist, but now rising star and dreamy bad girl Brooklyn Shaw is a threat both to Eden's title and her heart. (978-1-63555-820-3)

The Last First Kiss by Julie Cannon. Kelly Newsome is so ready for a tropical island vacation, but she never expects to meet the woman who could give her her last first kiss. (978-1-63555-768-8)

The Mandolin Lunch by Missouri Vaun. Despite their immediate attraction, everything about Garet Allen says short-term, and Tess Hill refuses to consider anything less than forever. (978-1-63555-566-0)

Thor: Daughter of Asgard by Genevieve McCluer. When Hannah Olsen finds out she's the reincarnation of Thor, she's thrown into a world of magic and intrigue, unexpected attraction, and a mystery she's got to unravel. (978-1-63555-814-2)

Veterinary Technician by Nancy Wheelton. When a stable of horses is threatened, Val and Ronnie must work together against the odds to save them and maybe even themselves along the way. (978-1-63555-839-5)

16 Steps to Forever by Georgia Beers. Can Brooke Sullivan and Macy Carr find themselves by finding each other? (978-1-63555-762-6)

All I Want for Christmas by Georgia Beers, Maggie Cummings & Fiona Riley. The Christmas season sparks passion and love in these stories by award-winning authors Georgia Beers, Maggie Cummings, and Fiona Riley. (978-1-63555-764-0)

From the Woods by Charlotte Greene. When Fiona goes backpacking in a protected wilderness, the last thing she expects is to be fighting for her life. (978-1-63555-793-0)

Heart of the Storm by Nicole Stiling. For Juliet Mitchell and Sienna Bennett a forbidden attraction definitely isn't worth upending the life they've worked so hard for. Is it? (978-1-63555-789-3)

If You Dare by Sandy Lowe. For Lauren West and Emma Prescott, following their passions is easy. Following their hearts, though? That's almost impossible. (978-1-63555-654-4)

Love Changes Everything by Jaime Maddox. For Samantha Brooks and Kirby Fielding, no matter how careful their plans, love will change everything. (978-1-63555-835-7)

Not This Time by MA Binfield. Flung back into each other's lives, can former bandmates Sophia and Madison have a second chance at romance? (978-1-63555-798-5)

The Found Jar by Jaycie Morrison. Fear keeps Emily Harris trapped in her emotionally vacant life; can she find the courage to let Beck Reynolds guide her toward love? (978-1-63555-825-8)